~~~~~~~~~~~~*The Scapegoat* ~~~~~~~~~~~~

The Scapegoat

Jocelyn Brooke

Afterword by

Peter Cameron

TURTLE POINT PRESS

NEW YORK

Turtle Point Press
© MCMXCVIII Jocelyn Brooke
First published by
The Bodley Head, London
1948

Library of Congress Catalog Number: 96-060142

ISBN: 1-885983-09-3

Acknowledgments are due to the Editor of
Orpheus I, in which certain passages
from this story first appeared.   — J.B.

Design and composition by
Wilsted & Taylor Publishing Services

Printed in the U.S.A.

PETER WARLOCK,
Folk-Song Preludes

Contents

PART ONE

Initiation

O N a late afternoon in December a train pulled up at a small country junction in the south-east of England. A single passenger — a soldier carrying full kit — waited on the platform. As soon as the train stopped he jumped into the nearest carriage, dragging his kitbag and pack in after him. Only when the train had begun to move did he notice that he had got into a first-class compartment, in which he was not entitled to travel. He noticed also, for the first time, that the carriage already contained another occupant: a boy of about thirteen with red hair, who was crouched in one of the corner seats farthest from the platform, his face wet with crying.

The brackish wintry light from outside mingled confusingly with the dim radiation of an electric bulb which had just been switched on; and in this vague illumination the figure of his travelling-companion produced upon the soldier an odd impression of insubstantiality. The man busied himself for some moments with his kit, unfastening the tight webbing-equipment and stowing it on top of the pack and kitbag on the luggage-rack. Then, with a sigh of relief, he sat down in the corner seat opposite his fellow-traveller.

Now that his eyes were becoming accustomed to the bewildering half-light, he could see clearly the smooth, pink-and-white flesh, smeared with tears, and the crown of rufous hair surmounting the paler orb of the face. The boy's appearance was oddly disquieting; there was about it a suggestion of hopelessness, a sense of utter surrender to some unhappiness which was felt to be inevitable and beyond the power of anybody to assuage.

"What's up, kid?" the soldier said at last, leaning slightly forward. "In trouble?"

"N-no," the boy replied unsteadily.

"You're O.K., then, are you?" the man pursued dubiously. He spoke with a strong Northumbrian accent.

"Y-yes," the boy echoed, hardly audible above the noise of the train.

"I suppose you live down these parts, eh?"

"No, I live at—in Devonshire. At least, I used to."

"Goin' to school, then, perhaps?" Even as he spoke, the soldier realized that the kid could hardly be going to school just now, a few days before Christmas. "Goin' away on a visit, like?" he suggested hopefully, wanting to say the right thing.

"No," the boy replied, rather more loudly. "I'm going to my uncle. I'm going to live with him."

"Live with your uncle, eh?" the soldier echoed.

"Y-yes. He lives at a place called Priorsholt, near Glamber."

"Oh, ay. I'm goin' to Glamber, too. Posted there. Cor, it's

been a hell of a journey — all the way from South Shields. Posted off leaf, I was."

"Are you going to live at Glamber?" the boy asked timidly. It was the first time he had spoken, except in answer to the other's questioning.

"I'll be stationed there." The soldier's voice took on a slightly "official" tinge — non-committal.

"My uncle lives in the country outside," the boy said, his voice gaining confidence.

"Well, you'll like that, I daresay. It'll be nice in summertime, anyway. Ain't you got no ma and pa?"

The boy's face crumpled up, and he suddenly began to cry again.

"My m-mother d-died," he gulped miserably.

The soldier, regretting his tactlessness, clicked his tongue apologetically.

"Sorry, kid — I didn't know. Was it just recently, then?"

"A m-month ago," the boy muttered.

"And you've lost your pa, too, eh?"

"He died ages ago — I can hardly remember him."

"Ah, that's bad. Well, you'll like living with your uncle in the country — that'll be all right, eh?" He spoke with a bluff, rather empty geniality.

"I — I — suppose so," the boy murmured, doubtfully.

The soldier lit a cigarette. In the flare of the match his face was suddenly revealed: rough and weather-worn, surmounted by a thatch of thick, dark hair, plastered down with grease. He was a big man of about thirty, heavily built, with the torso of a boxer.

After a pause, he leaned forward again — impelled partly by a feeling of pure compassion, partly by a more obscure motive: a compulsive desire, half-realized, to force the boy into a closer intimacy with himself.

"What do they call you, then?" he inquired.

The boy stared at him, puzzled.

"What's your moniker — your name, I mean?"

"Duncan," came the reply, uttered mechanically. "Duncan Cameron."

"One of the Jocks, eh? Mine's Tylor — Jim Tylor. I'm a Geordie, myself." He fumbled in his pocket, and at last produced a rather squashed bar of chocolate. "Here," he said, "have a bite."

Duncan ate the chocolate in silence; the afternoon light was thickening, and the carriage was filled with the dim yellow glow of the electric bulb. Presently, feeling a need to visit the lavatory, he went out into the corridor. When he had relieved himself he stumbled back along the swaying carriage, searching for the khaki-clad figure of his companion. But instead of entering the compartment, he stood in the corridor, staring vaguely out of the window at the unfamiliar country. He felt curiously reluctant to return to his seat opposite that of the soldier. The man's rough, unfamiliar speech disturbed him; and his whole

presence had for Duncan (who had never, so far as he could remember, spoken to a soldier before) an alien, rather frightening quality. At the same time he found this new acquaintance
curiously fascinating; and more than once, as he stood at the
window, he found himself peering round half furtively to look
again at the broad, muscular figure slumped heavily in the corner seat.

For some time the landscape had been hilly, the line running
between chalky uplands, sometimes bare, sometimes topped
with a crown of dark trees, or covered entirely with hanging
beech-woods. Now the train was running into flatter country:
the hills had retreated to the horizon, and level fields lay on
either side, criss-crossed with streams and dykes. Pollard wil-
lows stood in rows, like untidy, upturned mops; the water-
ways, reflecting the fading light, gleamed with a cold, steellike
brightness.

Leaning out of the window, careless of the soot which
lodged on his tear-wet cheeks, the boy inhaled the cold, salty
air, smelling already of the sea. Coming from the softer, more
feminine West Country, this eastern land seemed to him bleak,
inimical, with a quality of masculine hardness. Yet, as the cold,
bracing air lightened his sense of physical inertia, so the
thought of living in this land, with his uncle whom he scarcely
knew, stimulated him to a mood of arduous acceptance, a passionate desire to acclimatize himself to a new way of life.
Glancing once again at the figure in the corner seat, it seemed

to him that the soldier was a living symbol of that new existence, so exciting yet so frightening, towards which, every moment, the train was bringing him closer.

WITHIN the short space of a month the whole of his past life had become, for Duncan, curiously unreal. His mother had died suddenly during his first term at a public school; he had come home for the funeral to find his Uncle Gerald in charge of the proceedings, and had learnt that his mother had appointed her only brother (and only surviving relative) to be his guardian until he came of age.

He had returned to school after the funeral, knowing that the house was to be sold, and that he would probably never see it again: in future he would spend the holidays with his uncle, who was a comparative stranger to him. The routine of school-life dulled his grief, or, more exactly, held it in suspension: the life was still so strange to him that all his energies were employed in the task of adaptation. Only now, coming back for the holidays, did his sorrow reassert itself; recurring intermittently, in sudden onsets of pain, like an aching tooth. It was perhaps as well that he was not returning to his old home: the prospect of a new life among strange and possibly unfriendly surroundings, desolate as it seemed, did at least spare him the painful impact of familiar things, which would have fed his unhappiness unbearably. Instead, his grief remained to some extent repressed, as it had done at school after his mother's death:

thrust to the margins of his consciousness by the imminence of a new life to which he would soon have to begin once again to adapt himself.

When he thought of his uncle, with whom he was to make his home, he was filled with a vague sense of dread, mingled with a feeling of adventurous excitement. He had seen Uncle Gerald perhaps half a dozen times since he could remember; in memory he emerged as a somewhat overwhelming personality, enormous and rather clumsy, not unkind, but indefinably alarming. Gerald's rare visits to his sister's house had always been treated by her as a sort of joke, like the reception of some half-savage potentate at a western Court. Duncan retained a peculiarly physical memory of these unaccustomed masculine invasions; the heavy, silver-backed hairbrushes, the strops and boot-trees, the smell of tobacco, of polished leather, and of an expensive brand of brilliantine.

This impact of masculinity had seemed more than normally outlandish in his mother's household, which for a long time had been inviolably feminine, and where, till he went away to school, he had lived in almost total ignorance of the ordinary appurtenances of manhood. His father, a country solicitor of some standing, had died almost before he could remember; and his widow, left adequately provided for, had led a lonely, self-sufficient life, devoted to the care of her son, and content, for the rest, with such small amenities as the neighbourhood afforded.

When he thought of his home, Duncan was apt often to think of it as a kind of remote, enchanted castle, like the Lady of Shalott's, magnificently aloof from the life surrounding it: an illusion fostered commonly enough by English middle-class households, especially when the masculine element is absent. Duncan's mother had surrounded herself with the atmosphere of a cosy, rather vitiated culture: pretty chintzes and cretonnes, second-rate water-colours, middle-brow novels, Spiritualism — the latter, in her widowhood, being little more than an act of piety towards her dead husband, who had been a zealous adherent of the cult.

Rather "delicate" and nervous, probably owing to an early attack of cerebro-spinal fever, Duncan had accepted, without question, his mother's somewhat unenterprising scale of values. As a day-boy at a local preparatory school, his attachment to the ambience of home had been scarcely disturbed; and the sudden plunge into the life of a public school (to which he had been sent at the instigation of his uncle) was more than normally a shock to him: dislocating, in fact, so irremediably his attachment to home, that his mother's death, occurring when it did, seemed almost irrelevant; so far had he travelled in six weeks from that mental climate in which her presence had seemed all-important.

His "nervousness" had made him an easy prey to a series of obsessions which had overtaken him between the ages of six and thirteen. His mother had been rather alarmed at the passionate intentness with which he had thrown himself into the hobby of the moment — botany, tame ferrets, "Frog" aeroplanes, home-made fireworks — but no discouragement, however tactful, had the slightest effect upon him. The obsession would at length burn itself out, to be succeeded by another. At one time he had conceived a horror of anything resembling the shape of an acorn: the brass knobs on his bed were of this form, and for weeks he was unable to sleep, until at last the bed was replaced by another.

At about the same time he had invented a race of fantastic creatures which he called "wild soldiers" — wild as opposed to the domesticated species. Small khaki figures, with the white scuts of rabbits, they inhabited a certain shrubbery of laurestinus in the garden, and for the period of his obsession he would haunt the shrubbery for hours at a time, armed with a large butterfly-net. Later, he had developed a naïve interest in Spiritualism, with his mother's rather half-hearted encouragement, and his study of the subject had tended to accentuate the difficulty which he found in distinguishing between reality and phantasy.

The plunge into school-life, followed by his mother's death, had produced in him an emotional disorientation, a shifting of values, which made his grasp of reality even more precarious. Staring, now, from the train window, at the unfamiliar and vaguely hostile landscape, it seemed to him that the conscious, feeling part of himself had been actually wrenched from his body, and now hung suspended in mid-air, like the reflection of the electric bulb above his head, somewhere out in the bleak grey twilight. The country, too, seemed curiously unreal: probably by some trick of the gradient, or the course which the line was taking, the hills and woods seemed to advance and retreat, to melt into strange shapes, to disappear and reappear with a bewildering inconsistency.

Turning away, at last, from the window, Duncan went back to the compartment and sat down opposite the soldier, who greeted him with a nod and a friendly grin.

"Old enough to smoke fags?" he inquired, holding out a pack of cigarettes towards Duncan.

Duncan, who had never smoked a cigarette in his life, took one almost without thinking. The soldier's whole personality had about it a strange quality of compulsion: his unexpected offer seemed to Duncan a kind of order which could not be disobeyed. Once again he was acutely aware of the frightening imminence of his new life; the smoking of the cigarette seemed a ceremony of initiation, a solemn act performed at the behest of one empowered, by some sudden and mysterious decree, to enforce it.

The cigarette was a Woodbine, and when the soldier lit it for him, Duncan began to cough. His head swam, and after the first puff or two, he felt slightly sick. He continued, however, to puff at it with determination, staring boldly across at his new friend. The pungent flavor of the cigarette seemed to him a concentrated essence of that fainter, more diffused odour which exhaled from the soldier himself—an alien, mysterious smell, partly tobacco, partly the warm body-reek of sweat and stale urine; to Duncan it seemed the very odour of heroism, an exhalation from the battlefield.

"Soon be there now," the soldier remarked, looking out of the window. Duncan followed his eyes: the hills seemed to be closing in again, and the tang of the sea became more noticeable. The train roared into a tunnel; when it emerged, the suburbs of the town were visible: red bungalows, a gasometer, a straggling road fringed with hoardings, petrol-stations, cafés. Leaning far out the boy could see, ahead, a smudged greyness of many houses, a church spire, a clear sea-washed sky patched with ravelled fragments of inky cloud. Then, as the line curved, the sea itself came into view: a steely-grey wall against the fading brightness. Beyond the town a headland jutted out into the channel, topped by the thin column of a lighthouse.

The train slowed, running into the station, and Duncan felt a sudden spasm of fear: a sense, almost, of immediate danger. Craning out of the window, he looked for his uncle, who was to meet him: and at last caught sight of him, standing by the barrier in a belted mackintosh, hatless, a riding-crop grasped firmly in his right hand. Tall, massively built, he seemed to dominate the crowded station, producing in Duncan the sense of some inescapable fatality. He had not remembered that his uncle was quite so large: looming beneath the station-lights, he seemed a colossus, pregnant with a dark and minatory power.

WAITING on the darkening platform in the shrewd easterly wind, Gerald March slapped his riding-crop repeatedly, with angry violence, against this thighs; he was in an extremely bad temper. The wind was cold, the train late; a parcel which should have arrived by rail a week ago had not come, or had been lost in transit. But these were mere straws, piled for good measure upon the heavier load which oppressed him.

He strode up and down, in a measured beat of a few yards, like a policeman: six feet four and almost disproportionately broad, he made a commanding and rather impressive figure — or so he liked to believe, and in fact most people who didn't know him too well would have agreed with him. At forty-five, he had kept the beefy youthfulness of an ex-Rugger player; he was openly proud of the fact, and extremely sensitive about any reference to his age. At the same time, he was secretly, unhappily aware of being past his prime: his body had begun to protest at last against a too-long-protracted boyishness; the greying hair proclaimed the fact to the world, and in private before the mirror, the fold in the belly, the slackening pectoral muscle, told their tale.

Passing the cloakroom he heard the porter (whom he had just scolded) inquiring about the parcel for "the Colonel." The courtesy-title pleased him: he had retired from the Army with the rank of major two years before, when his father had died, and he had inherited what he commonly referred to as the "estate." Like his colonel's rank, the estate was little more than a courtesy-title: his inheritance, apart from a not very valuable share in his grandfather's business and a few rather dubious investments, consisted of a small converted farm-house and a farm of two hundred acres, which his father had bought on his retirement and run as a hobby for a time; finally letting the land to a tenant, who had consistently mismanaged it for a number of years. But people still spoke of "the Colonel's estate," much to Gerald's satisfaction. Accepted by what remained of the few county families in the district, but not especially popular with them, he was glad of such props to his social status. He had served with a good regiment, his family had been to the same public school for two or three generations, but the fact remained, his grandfather had been in the timber-trade; they were not "county," and Gerald, whose brother-officers had mostly answered, if only approximately, to the coveted description, was extremely sensitive on the point.

He had resigned his commission with the intention of settling down as a country gentleman, and perhaps running the farm as a side-line like his father before him. As things turned out, however, the best he could hope for was to be a gentleman-farmer. He realized soon enough that his father's tenant had brought the farm near to ruin. Nothing, it appeared, but unlimited capital — or perhaps unlimited hard work — could save it. The tenant, lazy and a drunkard, was easily bought out; but the transaction was an expensive one, and after two years of unremitting labour, Gerald saw little prospect of realizing his ambition — which was to sell off the farm as soon as he could, and settle down on the proceeds to a life of modest (but gentlemanly) ease. He had even begun, lately, to regret leaving the Army, for with the likelihood of an imminent war the prospects of promotion were brighter than for many years.

And now, to add to his misfortunes, his sister had died and appointed him her son's guardian. Not that this was, financially, a disadvantage: Arabella had been fairly well-off, and her son's future was provided for. A sum had been laid aside to cover his school-fees and other expenses; the residue, at present held in trust, he would inherit when he came of age. Should he predecease his uncle — an unlikely event, though the boy was supposed to be delicate — the estate would revert to Gerald. In addition, Arabella had been generous, and her brother had received a legacy of a thousand pounds.

No, financially the situation was no worse: what irked him was the responsibility of making a home for the boy. Gerald, at forty-five, had a deep-rooted horror of being what he privately referred to as "caught." A bachelor, he had for most of his life successfully avoided entanglements, emotional or otherwise.

He had been "caught" once by the farm; and now he was caught again, doubly caught. He couldn't refuse the guardianship of Arabella's boy, and he was bound to make some sort of home for him. Not that he had been particularly attached to his sister; but he had a strong sense of family duty, and there seemed no way out of it. He had disapproved of Arabella's marriage in the first place; still more strongly had he disapproved of her upbringing of Duncan. The boy should have been sent to a proper prep. school, as a boarder, at the normal age; but Arabella would never hear of it. She had agreed, after much argument, to send him to a public school (though she cherished a weakness for some place called Bedales); but Gerald considered that the concession had come too late, and he had washed his hands of the affair. He could hardly foresee that Arabella would die when she did (though for that matter one might have expected something of the kind, with all that faith-healing nonsense); or that, dying, she would bequeath to himself the full weight of a responsibility which, even in a mitigated form, he had lately been careful to decline.

Still, the deed was done: he was "caught" — properly caught. Anyway, Gerald reflected, we'll have to try and make a man of him; as far as the boy himself was concerned, it might be the making of him. He'd had too much of Arabella's silliness, no doubt. One might even manage to get him into Sandhurst.

At last, the train pulled in, and Gerald searched the line of windows for the half-remembered face. Yes, there he was:

carrot-haired, white-faced — not a bad-looking kid, but unhealthy. Looks like a girl, Gerald thought; and as he stepped forward to the carriage, he saw that the kid had obviously been crying. More soft-hearted than he liked to imagine, he felt a strong impulse of sympathy for the boy: after all, he had lost his mother. At the same time, mingled with his sympathy, he felt a peculiar disquiet, almost like a premonition of misfortune. Duncan's face (the train had stopped now) looked oddly immaterial, ghost-like, in the uncertain light, filling Gerald with an obscure sense of complexity, a feeling that the situation was less simple than it seemed. . . . Ridiculous, he thought, brushing the idea aside; I'm getting "nervy." Must be all the war-talk you heard nowadays: the "war of nerves" as they called it.

As Duncan stepped on to the platform, Gerald greeted him with genial affection.

"Hullo, kiddo," he said. "Glad to see you. I've got the old bus outside. We'll just collect your luggage, shall we?" Grasping the boy's arm, he hurried him along towards the luggage-van: Duncan, meanwhile, craning backwards over his shoulder to look for his soldier-friend, to whom he had forgotten to say good-bye; but the soldier, while Duncan was greeting his uncle, had moved off towards the barrier, and was already out of sight.

HUDDLED beside his uncle in the front of the battered, mud-stained Morris, Duncan hardly replied to Gerald's kindly meant questions and remarks. The sense of danger which had assailed him as the train pulled in, persisted: and as each new impression impinged on his senses, he felt more acutely than ever that he had arrived in an alien land. In his nostrils the smell of wet mackintosh and leather mingled with the alkaline tang of the sea, impressing him afresh with strangeness. The bourgeois seaside-town, sliding past in the thickening dusk, seemed unfriendly: solid, sham-Georgian houses behind laurels, with spiky gates. As they passed through the poorer quarter, a child ran across the street, and when Gerald slammed the brakes on, a woman screamed at them angrily, and a group of soldiers standing at the corner laughed and shouted obscenities.

Meanwhile Gerald kept up a one-sided, rather gusty conversation: "Hope you'll settle down all right—not what you've been used to, exactly, of course; but if you like the country, and country sort of things, you'll be O.K. . . . 'Fraid you'll have to rather make your own amusements. . . . Fact is, I'm hellish busy at the moment. . . . Bitten off more than I can chew. . . . Can't afford to take on any more labour. . . . Done any riding? You ought to take to it—we can fix you up with something. . . . There, we're out of that blasted town. You'll be able to see the house in a sec, once we're up this hill."

The car breasted a steep flank of down, treeless, sharp-edged against the western sky. Presently the road dipped again, revealing a more domesticated country of small valleys and wooded hills.

"Look—you can see the house now: those lights, below there."

Dimly, lights showed in the valley, beneath a humped mass

of woodland. The house appeared in vague outline; at the side, a short distance from the house itself, stood a group of extra-ordinary shapes; to Duncan they seemed like the figures of enormous women in cowled head-dresses, overtopping the house: figures of a dream, gigantic and menacing.

"What are those — those" — surely they must be buildings after all — "those chimney-things?" Duncan asked.

"Oh, the oast-houses. I suppose you don't get 'em in your part of the country. For drying hops. Don't go in for hops much, myself — not enough land to spare. The oasts date from when the farm was a much bigger concern. . . . No, fruit's more in my line: I want to go in for it in a big way."

At last the car pulled up before the house. Little could be seen of it in the darkness: a row of gables appeared indistinctly against the sky, suggesting the form of an enormous bat's wing. Duncan followed his uncle through the open door. Sims, Ger-ald's ex-soldier-servant, carried in the luggage. A dourly good-looking man, he smiled in a rather guarded way at Duncan.

"He's my main stand-by," Gerald explained. "Does most of the housework, cooks, does any odd job. I haven't much use for women about the place, myself. We have to have a daily girl from the village, but you can't get 'em to sleep in nowadays."

The door led into an entrance-hall which apparently in-cluded sitting-room and dining-room. A fire of oak-boughs burnt sulkily in the grate, and a table was laid for a meal. Ger-ald's father had bought the house after his wife's death, and since the Marches had been in possession it had been exclusively a house of men. No feminine elegancies relieved the austere masculinity of the room. There were leather chairs, piperacks, ash-trays, foxes' masks, an assortment of horns: the only pictures were a few sporting prints and football groups. Half-consciously Duncan found himself looking for a single homely touch—flowers, loose covers, cushions, anything to soften the room's austerity—but found none. Gerald had shared with his father a taste for masculine comfort without frills; it would no more have occurred to him (for instance) to have flowers in a room, than to use scent, or to have his nails manicured.

Duncan, sorting out his baggage, looked up questioningly at his uncle. He was impressed again, as he had been at the station, by his enormous size: the room was a large one, but seemed scarcely big enough to contain its owner with comfort.

Gerald grinned amicably.

"I expect you're hungry," he said. "I'll show you up to your room, and then we'll feed."

His voice and manner were purely friendly, yet Duncan still had a disquieting sense of lurking danger. Out of the corner of his eye, as he bent over the suit-cases, he studied Gerald's face. Broad, healthily tanned, of a tough, leathery texture, there was nothing extraordinary about it. When he smiled, his lips opened squarely, like a trapdoor, beneath the small bristly moustache, revealing a set of sound, regular teeth. His dark hair, thinning on top and beginning to turn grey, was cropped extremely short at the back and sides, and this gave his large, well-shaped head a peculiarly naked appearance.

"Ready? Come on then, we'll go up. You're sleeping in what used to be my dressing-room. We thought it'd be less lonely for you there at first.

It was, as a matter of fact, Arabella's housekeeper who had thought it would be "less lonely"; she had taken Gerald aside after the funeral and spoken of Duncan's "nerves." "He's hardly used to sleeping quite alone," she had explained. "Ours is a small house, and he's always been within call. He's better now than he used to be, but seeing as he's going to a strange house, if you could put him somewhere near you. . . ." And Gerald, who privately thought that "nerves" were all rot in a boy of thirteen, had obediently had a bed made up in the small room leading out of his own bedroom.

"Hope you'll be comfortable. . . . Shouldn't bother to unpack much tonight. . . . The bathroom's just across the passage — the rear's next door. Come down when you're ready, and I'll tell Sims to buck up with the supper."

The small room was bare as a monk's cell: a bed, a chair, a bedside table, nothing else. Duncan unpacked a few necessities, and went to have a wash. He moved with careful deliberation, trying to quell the disturbance in his mind. But it was as though a crowd of people surrounded him, all giving him contradictory advice. The most trivial action was fraught with indecision. He took up a toothbrush to brush his hair, the soap slipped from his hand and could not be found, the towel fell into the basin.

At last, wearily, he went to the window and looked out. Very faintly the humped wood showed against the sky. A light gleamed dimly from some cottage immediately opposite. As he stood looking out, he fancied that he heard a curious singing noise, an indeterminate droning like the noise in a sea-shell. Probably it was some trick of the wind, or merely that he was extremely tired. . . . He turned from the window, and reluctantly prepared to join his uncle. Passing through the large bedroom, he recognized the heavy, valuable-looking toilet articles — the razor-strop, boot-trees, silver brushes. A camel-hair dressing-gown hung over a chair, and a pair of rather old-fashioned "frogged" pyjamas was laid out ready for the night. On the wall hung several regimental groups: one included Gerald, in Rugger-kit, glowering angrily at the camera. Duncan remembered that he had once played Rugger for the Army.

He turned away rather hopelessly and, sick with fatigue and nostalgia, a stranger in enemy country, made his way slowly downstairs.

three

N EXT morning Duncan was awakened before dawn
by the farm noises: lowing of cows, clanking buckets, distant shouts and laughter as the men went to
work. The window-space was dark as midnight still; Duncan
turned over and tried to close his mind against those morning-
sounds which heralded, like the faint introductory notes of an
overture, the first day of his new life.

He was not, however, to be left in peace for long. Soon he
saw, beneath the door, Gerald's light switched on; and a moment later Gerald himself threw the door open and bounced in.
His enormous body, in the elaborate frogged pyjamas, exhaled
an overmastering, a rather monstrous vitality. To Duncan, his
sudden apparition seemed portentous, disturbing as a bugle-
blast.

"I'm just going to have my bath," he announced. "I have a
cold one myself, but no doubt you're used to a hot one. I'll run
it for you, if you like. Nip along in about ten minutes, and it'll
be ready for you. I'm afraid we get up early here — I have to turn
out to see after the men."

Duncan sat up, suddenly wide-awake, meeting his uncle's

dark, portentous eyes. Gerald's pyjama-jacket was unbuttoned, and in the middle of his smooth white chest was a lozenge-shaped patch of black hair.

"I take it you'll have a hot one, eh?" he repeated, pausing in the doorway. Liable by nature to be bad-tempered before breakfast, his face was sullen, and his voice had an overbearing, almost a bullying tone; though his words were friendly enough.

Duncan lowered his eyes, suddenly embarrassed.

"I'll have a cold one," he said.

"That's a good lad — much healthier," Gerald exclaimed breezily. "Don't be too long."

He left the room as violently as he had entered it, banging the door. With a blessed sense of respite, Duncan pulled the clothes over his head and drew his knees up to his chin, as though by concealing himself and making himself as small as possible he could exclude, if only for a few minutes, the new life which, like a raw, unaccustomed climate, awaited him outside the small kingdom of his bed.

Drowsily, but with a deliberate effort to escape from the imminence of what lay before him, he urged himself farther and farther into the remote territories of his own imagination, till at last he reached the innermost sanctuary, the inviolable province of his most private phantasy. This ultramontane country, visited irregularly, was of a variable landscape, but its most usual aspect was that of a South-Sea island, blessed with perpetual fine weather, and having a sandy beach, a lagoon, a roughly built log-cabin — all the paraphernalia, in fact, of *Coral Island* (which was Duncan's favourite book, except for *Mr. Tod*); but with this advantage, that the population was of his own choosing. Or so, at least, he had always imagined; on his last visit the inhabitants had consisted of the head-boy at his day-school, and — a recent immigrant — one of the younger masters from his public school. This morning the personnel had changed: he recognized the soldier whom he had met in the train and, to his intense surprise, his Uncle Gerald — attired, rather unsuitably, in Rugger-kit, and glaring sullenly before him as he had glared from the photograph in the bedroom. Duncan saluted him gravely: once ashore on the island, his right to be there could not be questioned. His presence was in itself a passport; he would remain there for as long as he chose, a naturalized citizen of a world existing beyond the bounds of space and time.

In spite of himself, Duncan fell into a brief doze. He woke again suddenly a few moments later, and leapt from the bed, stricken with guilt at his defection. The prospect of the cold bath made him shudder: he had scarcely ever had one in his life. But he was filled now with a curious, deliberate valour, a determination to come to terms in the most direct way possible with this naked, heroic life which was henceforward to be his.

On his way through his uncle's room, he paused for an instant to look again at the photograph of the Rugger-group.

Gerald, his immense thighs bulging from exiguous shorts, frowned back at him sternly and compellingly: as though urging him to the fulfilment of some inexorable duty.

Hurrying across to the bathroom, hardly doubting that he was late, and that his uncle had already gone down to breakfast, he threw open the door, and was startled to see Gerald, stark naked, towelling himself energetically before the open window.

An habitual modesty made Duncan duck his head and make as though to back out of the room.

"I'm sorry — I thought — "

"All right, all right, come in," Gerald shouted. "I haven't run your bath yet — it won't take two minutes, though."

He draped his towel round his waist, and leaned over the bath, replacing the plug and turning on the cold tap.

Duncan leaned against the door, still embarrassed by his uncle's nakedness. Excessively modest himself, he was reluctant to intrude on the intimacies of others. Naked, Gerald seemed more preternaturally enormous than ever; Duncan eyed nervously the white, heavily muscled body, compelled to a sort of unwilling reverence for the power latent in those massive yet agile limbs.

Gerald, who had started to shave, glanced at Duncan with a smile of quizzical friendliness.

"What's up? Admiring my manly torso, or something?"

Duncan blushed scarlet, and leaned over to turn off the

bath-tap. The bath was already almost half-full. Turning back towards his uncle, he said, "You're very strong, aren't you?"

Gerald grunted, non-committally.

"I'm not so young as I was, that's the trouble," he grumbled. He patted his belly, and looked himself over, critically, but with a certain pride. "I'll be running to fat soon."

He turned away and continued his shaving. Duncan lingered in his pyjamas, unable to screw himself up to the ordeal of the icy water; he was shy, moreover, of stripping naked before his uncle.

"Don't wait for me," Gerald shouted over his shoulder. "You'll get cold standing about." Himself, he seemed impervious to cold. Naked before the window, he might have been in a Turkish bath for all the discomfort which he exhibited. Suddenly he burst into a raucous snatch of song: his voice was unexpectedly coarse, and its callow, vibrant tones, assaulting the morning silence, affected Duncan with a peculiarly unpleasant sensation, as though his uncle had uttered some indecent remark.

Unable to think of an excuse for further delay, Duncan began to take off his pyjamas. As he slipped his trousers from his waist, his uncle glanced round again.

"You're shivering," he observed. "Won't do to catch cold, you know. . . . We'll have to toughen you up a bit. It wouldn't be a bad plan to do a few jerks each morning, you know. This sort of thing." He put down the razor and flexed his arms. "Up, forward, sideways, down. Warm you up in no time."

Reluctantly, standing naked before his uncle's towering body, with its flexed, bulging muscles, Duncan forced himself to follow his movements, synchronizing his own with extreme clumsiness. He noticed that his uncle had cut himself shaving, and that the bright blood had dripped on to his chest, making a zigzag scarlet streak across the white skin.

"That's the idea—put a bit more into it, though." Gerald paused, turning away suddenly to dab his bleeding face. "Put on you pants if you like. . . ." When Duncan had pulled on his pyjama-trousers, he turned round again. "O.K. We'll start again. That's better. Up, sideways, forward—that's the stuff. Looks as if you could do with a bit more muscle on you. You've not got a bad body, though. We might make a horseman of you one day. . . . You want to get those shoulders back. . . ." He stepped forward, and with both hands forced back Duncan's shoulders. "Keep your back straight. That's better. Now touch your toes with your fingers. . . . O.K. that'll do for today. Now buck up and have your bath."

Rapidly, with an intense determination, Duncan pulled off his trousers, and, holding his breath, plunged full length into the bath. Then he soaped himself carefully, trying hard to conceal his shivering. Setting his teeth, he lay down once again at full length, forcing himself to remain submerged for fully half a minute.

"That'll do," Gerald exclaimed at last. "Better get out now and have a good rub down."

Grateful for the deliverance, Duncan stepped out and began

to dry himself. Gerald, who had finished shaving, was scrambling into his underclothes—Aertex shorts and a singlet.

"Okeydoke, kid," he grinned, as he moved towards the door. "We'll soon have you fit as a fiddle, if you keep it up."

Banging the door behind him, he bounced across to the bedroom, where Duncan could hear him singing lustily as he dressed.

When he had dried himself, Duncan observed that his uncle had left his razor on the window-ledge. It was a cut-throat of old-fashioned pattern: in his toilet-articles and many of his clothes Gerald was inclined to cling to outdated modes. Curiously, Duncan picked up the razor; it slipped in his hand, and he cut himself slightly. The bright blood, splashing suddenly on the white enamelled basin, startled him. A drop had fallen on the blade of the razor, and he was about to wipe it off, but suddenly decided to leave it; he could not have explained why, but the decision was accompanied by a curious feeling of pleasure.

Back in his room, he looked out at the bright, wintry morning. The woods lay still and silent in the early sun. Vaguely Duncan found himself looking for the house or cottage whose light he had seen the night before; it should have been exactly opposite his window, on the steepest part of the hillside. No house, however, was visible. The wood was thin at that point, and any building, however small, must have shown up clearly. Surprised, he turned away and began to dress.

four

A T breakfast, Duncan asked his uncle about the light in the wood: the absence of any obvious explanation had set up a kind of reverberation of anxiety in his mind. Gerald, when he heard the question, shot a curious look at him: for a moment, it almost seemed as if he were embarrassed.

"There's no house there — on the hillside. Nearest one's the keeper's cottage, and that's a couple of miles away. . . . Nobody would be out in the wood at that time of night, unless it was a poacher — and a poacher would hardly carry a light. No — you must have been seeing things." He laughed, and his expression was so frank and normal, that Duncan mentally discounted what had seemed his "embarrassment" of a moment before. He must, he realized, have been mistaken; there was something about Gerald's manner, he thought, which made it easy to misunderstand him.

After breakfast, Gerald suggested a tour of the farm. "Might as well get the lie of the land," he said. Secretly, Gerald was rather looking forward to showing off the farm to someone who would not be too critical.

In front of the house were the relics of a garden: a square of neglected lawn, surrounded by unweeded flower-beds and un-pruned rambler-roses.

"No time for flower-gardening," Gerald explained. "You might take a turn at it, if you care for that sort of thing."

They paused to look up at the house: faced with grey ce-ment, it appeared an undistinguished, mid-Victorian struc-ture, decent and homely, but lacking in charm.

"Parts of it are old, though you'd not think it. Fourteenth century. It's all been built round at different times. They say the name — Priorsholt — has something to do with an abbey or priory or something that lay just near. I've never been into all that myself. No time. The pater had some odd sort of theories. Interested in history and all that. I've never had time for it."

Gerald laughed, but Duncan had an odd impression that he was dropping the subject rather quickly. For a moment, his face wore the expression which Duncan had noticed — or thought he had noticed — when he mentioned the mysterious light.

The morning was cold and clear, with a high pale sky. Twigs and leaves were fledged with rime, and ice lay thinly on the cart-tracks and puddles. Beyond the garden, fields fell away to the left; to the right, a track bordered by a tall hedge, interspersed with hollies and yew-trees, led up the hillside to where the woods began.

"Here are the cowsheds, you see," Gerald explained. "Still in need of repair, I'm afraid. The cowman's O.K., but he's al-ways telling me how the other bloke ran things. Conservative

lot, the farm-people round here. I think we'll go round by Forty
Acres — I want to have a look at that wheat Jarvis was talking
about. And then you'll be able to see where I want to plant out
my new orchards. It's time that Wychwood field was grassed
down, too — it's been no bloody good since I can remember."

Duncan listened with intense concentration, following at
his uncle's side. They made a complete tour of the farm, Gerald
talking without interruption, referring constantly to people,
things and places of which Duncan could obviously never have
heard. After two hours of it, he had talked himself into a mood
of extraordinary joviality. His mood infected Duncan, who was
flattered at being talked to as a grown-up and an equal; moreover, having habituated himself since his mother's death to expect the worst of his uncle, he was apt to over-value the least
show of kindness or flattery, construing it as a sign of genuine
friendship, even of love. And now that Gerald was an inhabi-
tant of the Island, he would have been, in any case, predisposed
in his favour.

Walking round the farm, listening to the endless flow of his
uncle's talk, Duncan felt a renewal of his determination to
come to terms with this alien yet exciting world of which Gerald, with his bouncing athleticism, was the despotic and exclu-
sive ruler. He recognized in himself the first symptoms of one
of his obsessional attachments; but in this case, the affair promised to be on an altogether larger scale. It was as though his previous "crazes," as his mother used to call them, had been the

preparatory stages in a process which was now nearing its logical conclusion. The ferrets, the fireworks, the rabbit-scutted
soldiers in the shrubbery, had been, as it were, a series of re-
hearsals, incomplete or abortive attempts at the real thing. The
process had begun, he realized, when he went to school last
September; but it was Gerald's presence on the "Island" that
had finally revealed the course which he was destined to take.

In the light of his new knowledge, the details of the farm-
work, as Gerald explained them, took on a magical significance;
Gerald's whole conversation, in fact, was a perpetual incantation, binding him ever more securely in his new and self-
imposed captivity — a captivity which, though he desired it and
sought to hasten its completion, was yet fraught with a strange
dread, a prescience of unimaginable danger.

Gerald continued to chatter amiably. The fact was, he had
been suffering lately from the lack of a good listener. Men of
his own class were few in the district, and those who would listen to him without interruption, fewer still. Gerald seldom
went far afield in search of society; once a month or so he would
spend a week-end in London, but even in London he had lost
touch with many of his friends. Duncan, in fact, was the first
person he had been able to talk to for a considerable time who
possessed the twin advantages of not being a farmhand or a servant, and not interrupting.

They came to the stables, and inspected Gerald's two horses:

Blackshirt, an ageing, seldom-used hunter, and a pony which, in a fit of extravagance, Gerald had recently bought.

"Like to take up riding?" Gerald asked. "This pony would just suit you nicely."

Once again, as when his uncle had suggested the cold bath, Duncan found himself compelled, with a curious and rather exciting sense of abandonment to his destiny, to assent; though he was, in fact, terrified of horses, and had never ridden or wanted to ride in his life before.

Gerald looked pleased.

"Good," he said. "We'll have you riding like Steve Donoghue before the end of the hols. Let's see now — I've got one or two jobs to do this morning; I could take you out this afternoon, though. How'd you like that?"

Duncan's heart sank: he had not been prepared to face the ordeal at quite such short notice.

"I — I haven't got any clothes," he murmured.

"Oh, that's all right," Gerald exclaimed. "Sims has got an old pair of bags that ought to fit you more or less — good enough to start with, anyway. We'll have to get you fitted out with some of your own next time we're in Glamber. O.K., then — I'll take you out after lunch."

He grinned, and gave Duncan's arm an affectionate squeeze.

"I'll have to go indoors for a bit now," he added. "Think you can amuse yourself till lunch-time?"

He moved away towards the house, walking with a slight swagger. He felt in an extraordinarily good temper. Riding would do his nephew a world of good, he thought; and he was looking forward to teaching him. There was about the boy a certain softness, an air of incompleteness like a half-finished sculpture: he needed moulding, Gerald decided — mentally and physically.

"We'll make a man of him yet," Gerald told himself; and the decision produced in him a peculiarly intense excitement, almost like that which accompanies some act of creation. For Gerald, indeed, the prospect of "making a man of" Duncan did seem, precisely, a creative act: in part, perhaps, a compensation for that act of generation which it seemed unlikely now that he would ever perform. For Gerald was one of those men who cherish an intermittent desire for fatherhood, though without wishing to saddle himself with the responsibilities of marriage.

LEFT alone, Duncan felt a sudden sinking of the heart. A moment before, his whole being had been concentrated, with a conscious and laborious marshalling of his faculties, upon the task of appearing worthy in his uncle's eyes. Now, with Gerald's departure, the impulsion which had keyed him up for the past two hours to an unaccustomed alertness, subsided abruptly. With a sudden backwash of emotion, he knew only that he had lost his mother and his home, and that he was in a strange country, afraid and without protection.

The sky had become overcast, with a thin luminous film of cloud obscuring the sun. Duncan mooched unhappily round the derelict garden, and leaned over the front gate. He would have liked to go for a walk, but the country seemed unfriendly and forbidding. The silent brown mass of the wood impended heavily above the house, watchful and menacing; there was about it something ancient and still untamed: one could imagine, in some future time, the forests creeping back gradually to engulf the farm-lands, the scattered houses overgrown and subsiding, the whole countryside reverting, at last, to the old wealden jungle. To Duncan, the most innocent objects — a spade stuck in a flower-bed, a fallen, moss-grown garden-urn, the dried seed-capsules of a delphinium — were suddenly impregnated with a sense of fatality: their silent, reticent forms seemed to be signalling a note of warning.

In the hedge by the gate, a few spindle-berries lingered — it had been a mild autumn — wrinkled and withering, the orange seeds clinging precariously to their puce-coloured envelopes. Tears stung Duncan's eyes as he remembered that his mother had loved them. Under the hedge, nearby, some woolly pink heads of the winter-butterbur were showing through a carpet of dead leaves; stooping to pick one, he inhaled the familiar heliotrope scent, and a fresh spasm of tears crumpled his face.

He leaned over the gate, his eyes fixed on the distant woods. Presently a sound of heavy, regular footsteps in the road distracted him. A column of soldiers was coming round the corner: one of the battalions in training at the neighbouring barracks. Weighed down with the cumbrous webbing-equipment, sweating in spite of the cold, their raw, meat-red faces surly beneath steel-helmets, they passed heavily down the narrow lane. To Duncan, the soldiers seemed an integral part of the landscape, the indigenous fauna of an unexplored, unfriendly country. Half-consciously, he found himself searching the dull, uniform faces for his friend of the train; unlikely though it was that he should belong to this particular unit. From where he stood, he could flair the same faint odour which his fellow-traveller had made familiar to him: an animal, foxy scent, suggesting a way of life remote and primitive, conditioned by some cruel Mithraic discipline. The smell affected Duncan with a lively and personal distaste, like the flavour of onions, which he detested. Yet the soldiers seemed to him, by association perhaps with his friend of yesterday, to constitute a kind of challenge to his new-found resolutions. Watching the column out of sight, he felt his primary disgust modulated, in some remote cavern of his mind, into a peculiar and inadmissible pleasure.

Presently he summoned the courage to walk out of the gate. Once outside, he crossed the road without further hesitation, and began to walk up the track towards the woods. A light wind had risen, rattling softly in the leaves of the hollies which stood out blackly, like dark, glistening fires, against the neutral-tinted landscape. Otherwise, the country seemed extraordinarily silent. Soon the path entered the wood, leading straight ahead through thickets of brown, sodden bracken. A pheasant shouted discordantly in the undergrowth, close at hand, startling the heavy woodland silence, which after this brief disturbance immediately descended again, seeming more intense than before.

Duncan walked on for some minutes, then, as a sudden idea struck him, branched off to the right, between the close-growing hazels. It would be about here, he decided, that he had seen the mysterious light the evening before. . . . He searched for some minutes, expecting to come upon a pile of ashes and charred sticks, or perhaps (in spite of what his uncle had said) some small hut or cabin. There were, however, no signs of any human visitor, except for an empty cartridge-case, which Duncan absently picked up and stuffed in his pocket. A bleached rabbit-skull also caught his attention, and this, too, he collected.

Returning to the path, he continued farther into the wood, which continued monotonously on either side: hazel-thickets scattered with oaks or Spanish chestnuts. He scarcely knew how long he had been walking when the path took a sudden turn, and the wood — or at least this part of it — came to an end. Climbing a hurdle which barred the path's end, he found himself in a sloping field, surrounded on three sides by woodland, and on the fourth dipping abruptly to a winding valley, beyond which more woods fringed the skyline.

As he stood at the field's edge, wondering which way to go, he saw a human figure emerge from the wood close by. It was an old man—immensely old, with a patriarchal beard, his limbs twisted by rheumatism: probably some woodman or casual labourer from a neighbouring farm. He approached Duncan, and touched his cap.

"Mornin', sir. Nice mornin'."

He stood there, in no hurry to move on, it seemed; not looking at Duncan, but gazing across the field towards the valley.

"It's a bad place," he muttered, more to himself than to the boy.

"Bad?" Duncan queried.

The old man turned round, half-surprised at being overheard.

"Yes, a bad place. That there field—nought'd ever grow in 'er. They ploughed 'er up in the War, but it's bad land, no good to nobody. I could've told 'em, and saved 'em the trouble. I mind me grandfather sayin' it was a bad place: you couldn't get him to set foot on it, even." The old man paused, and shook his head.

Duncan, looking across the field, noticed for the first time, about fifty yards away, a curious structure: two roughly shaped stones standing upright, with another flattened stone lying horizontally across their summits. The whole was about ten feet tall. Duncan remembered pictures of Stonehenge, and supposed that this, too, was some prehistoric monument.

The old man had followed his eyes, and, as though to himself, muttered something indistinctly about "Them stones." He remained there, silent, for a few minutes longer. Then, as though his train of thought had come full circle, he repeated his original remark, "It's a bad place." Presently, with a polite "Good morning," he shambled off towards the path.

Curious to examine the stones, Duncan walked across the field towards them. The ground was rough, pitted with rabbit-holes, and clothed with the coarse, tufted taw-grass. Clumps of squalid, withering ragwort, lingering in late bloom, made patches of faded yellow. A stunted thornbush grew near the stones, bent level with the ground by the south-west winds.

A few yards from the stones Duncan stumbled over a rabbit-hole, and just saved himself from falling flat on his face. At his feet lay the remains of a dead sheep, far gone in rottenness. A gaping rent in the flesh revealed a pullulating mass of fat, whitish maggots.

Duncan started away, overcome by a sudden and extreme nausea. Turning in his tracks he stumbled back towards the homeward path. The old man's words seemed to him invested with a new and sinister significance: "It's a bad place." As he reached the hurdle he became suddenly aware of a confused noise; still preoccupied with the horrible thing in the field, his brain worked slowly, and he was only just in time to leap to safety as Gerald, galloping up the path on Blackshirt, cleared the hurdle, and landed in the field.

Seeing his nephew Gerald looked completely dumbfounded. His face went blank, his eyes gleaming darkly with a kind of angry bewilderment.

"What the devil are you doing here?" he shouted.

Duncan felt his mind swoon into an abyss of pure terror. It was true he had nearly been ridden down; but Gerald's tone and expression, his white-faced, burning anger, had a quality of terrifying irrelevance. To say the least, his violent outburst seemed wildly out of proportion to any perceptible cause; and coming after the encounter with the dead sheep, seemed to Duncan in some mysterious way connected with it, so that the vision of the rotted carcase, with its obscene swarm of maggots, recurred in all its horror, haloed, as it were, with the fiery aura of his uncle's meaningless fury.

"Why — what . . ." Duncan stammered. "I'm sorry I was in the way. I didn't . . ."

"Oh, all right, no offence." Gerald grinned, suddenly normal again. "You only startled me, rather, popping up like that." He paused. Then he made a curious remark, "I suppose you had to come here sooner or later." The words were uttered so low that Duncan, mistrusting his ears, asked, "What did you say?"

"Nothing. . . . What?" Gerald looked suddenly startled, as though roused from some private imagining.

"I thought you said something — I couldn't catch."

"No — I don't know. Forget now what I *did* say." He grinned again, all friendly. "Been looking at the old Druids' stones, eh? There's some old what-do-you-call-'ems, too, hereabouts — tumuli. Tombs of Danes or Saxons or something. Yes, there they are. . . ." He pointed with his crop to an opening in the wood, where three mounds, clothed with ivy and withering dog's-mercury, rose from the level, leafy floor.

Duncan looked, without much interest, at the tombs; he was anxious to get away from the place. The sunlight was now entirely obscured by thickening clouds: the country seemed to have gone dead, brooding in a silent, malevolent dream. Duncan, watching his uncle, half-fearing a fresh outburst, felt himself stiffening to withstand the assault of terror. Danger flickered over the woods like lightning. It was a bad place.

Gerald was staring vaguely across the field towards the stones. Suddenly he became alert: from the height of the saddle, he had perceived something which, at this distance, was invisible to Duncan.

"Something queer — I can't see . . ." he muttered, in a preoccupied tone.

Following his eyes, Duncan exclaimed, nervously, "It's a dead sheep."

"A what?" said Gerald sharply. Once again, his manner seemed to Duncan, oddly unsuited to the occasion: over-emphatic, and somehow rather frightening.

"A dead sheep," Duncan repeated, uneasily, possessed suddenly by an excruciating need to make water.

Gerald glared at him with what seemed a meaningless intensity: it was as though he had misheard his nephew's words, or as though, unknown to Duncan, the words themselves were invested with some sinister double-meaning. Suddenly Gerald turned away, with a peculiar air of embarrassment.

"Oh well, never mind," he laughed, with another sudden switch to joviality. "It's time we were getting back to lunch. D'you mind pulling the hurdle aside? I'm not going to take him over this time."

Duncan paused, when the horse had passed through, to urinate at the side of the path. He was rather embarrassed by his uncle's presence, and it was some minutes before he turned to accompany Gerald down the track. On horseback Gerald seemed more than ever monumental: he rode superbly, moulded like a centaur to the horse's body. His whole figure alert, the muscles flexed, he gave a curious impression of being too big for his clothes, as if his enormous body resented the impediment of whipcord and tweed.

Half-fearful, half-admiring, Duncan trotted at his side. A little way down the path, Gerald suddenly pulled up his horse.

"Look there!" He pointed upwards into the overhanging branches of a tree. Duncan saw an orbicular mass of green twigs—perhaps a rook's nest? He looked again.

"Why, it's mistletoe," he said. "I never noticed it."

"We'd better get some for Christmas," Gerald suggested. "Here, hold Blackshirt — it's all right, he won't bite you," With the agility of a circus-rider he stood up on the saddle, and swung himself bodily on to the branch, sitting it astride. It was a considerable feat for a man of forty-five. Duncan watched him admiringly, as he cut off the mistletoe with a jackknife, flung it on to the path, and then lowered himself, confidently, on to the saddle again.

Duncan handed him up the mistletoe; he took it, glanced at it with an expression of pleasure, then handed it back: presenting it to his nephew with an oddly eager, rather ceremonious air.

"Thank you very much," the boy murmured politely.

There was something strangely ceremonial about the whole incident: it was as though it were part of some ritual. Duncan was vaguely puzzled: Gerald's air, as he handed him the mistletoe, was almost apologetic — the expression of one who makes inadequate amends for some injury. The moment passed: Gerald laughed — rather as one who "laughs off" some unpleasant or embarrassing episode.

"I don't know who you'll find to kiss under it," he chuckled. "We don't run to pretty girls much, here."

Duncan laughed politely; but a vaguely disquieting idea was forming at the back of his mind. There were, it seemed to him, two Uncle Geralds: the normal, jovial, everyday personality, and the other, secret, menacing, given to sudden strange embarrassments and bursts of anger.

The "normal" Gerald was uppermost at the moment. He chatted and joked in his facile, amiable strain all the way back to the house. As before, Duncan found this attitude flattering, and he found it easy to forget, while Gerald's mood lasted, that other and darker aspect of his uncle which existed, so it seemed, behind the bluff, benevolent façade.

five

D
UNCAN'S first riding-lesson was probably the most frightening thing that had ever happened to him. A sense of disquiet pervaded the whole occasion; over and above the sheer physical effort, he was obscurely aware that the ordeal was crucial in a wider sense. It was not merely a question of staying in the saddle, or even of learning, ultimately, to ride; his whole existence, he felt, was in some way involved, the event marked a sort of climax in that process of initiation by which his personality was slowly but surely being subordinated to his uncle's, and all that his uncle stood for. The riding-lesson was a kind of test; if he passed it, he would have advanced a further stage — and an important one — in his progress towards complete identification with his uncle's world. There seemed to him, indeed, a certain finality about this particular stage in his journey: for there would be, he realized, no going back. If he "passed," he would belong irrevocably to this mysterious, unhomely life .of Priorsholt — the life of horses and foxes' masks, of Gerald's massive hairbrushes and frogged pyjamas, of cold baths and physical jerks in the morning. Repelled yet fascinated, he felt that the choice was no longer his: he was committed to the journey, and, once across the frontier, there

would be no question of changing his mind. The thought that it was already, probably, too late to turn back, was in itself strangely exciting; he remembered stories he had read of men who had sold themselves to the Devil, and he wondered, obscurely, if his own experience was of a similar nature.

WHERE riding was concerned, Gerald recognized no half-measures. Horsemanship was one of a very limited number of things which he took dead-seriously. His methods were those of the Army riding-school. Age, ability, previous experience made no difference whatever. Up on the downs, within sight of the barracks which marked the beginning of the town, he was no longer a gentleman-farmer teaching his nephew to ride, but an Army riding-master knocking hell out of a new recruit.

"For Christ's sake listen to what I'm telling you, and try and do it. Grip with your thighs. Keep your elbows in. Keep your toes *up*. . . . No, *don't* hold the reins like that. Look, watch me. Now you've lost your grip again. . . . Keep those bloody elbows in, for God's sake! Oh, Christ, man, *listen* when I tell you. . . . Now, try and rise to the trot. No, you'll never get it that way. . . . Don't give him his head too much — he's fresh, and you don't want to canter yet. . . . For God's sake, *grip*, man, grip with your thighs. Look, just watch me for a second."

Duncan, almost exhausted by the muscular strain and the effort of concentration, watched his uncle trot smartly by: elbows pressed to hips, thighs gripping the saddle with the ease of a handclasp, trunk erect. Alert with fatigue and apprehension, Duncan saw him with a singular clarity, almost as though he were seeing him for the first time: saw him, as it were, through a magnifying lens, larger than life, with every detail apparent. He noticed, in particular, the flesh of his neck, beneath the cropped greying hair, bulge and subside, as he rose with the trot, like a thong of leather above the tight collar. At one side, behind the ear, was the whitish, multiple scar of an old acne.

"Come on then—don't sit there half-asleep. Get cracking. Don't forget those elbows, now: there, that's better. You were rising to the trot then. Couldn't you feel the difference? No, no—you've lost it again. Watch me, for God's sake. . . ."

For two hours the ordeal continued. Round and round, backwards and forwards, Duncan trotted, the bitter east wind stinging his face, his body jolted and strained almost past bearing, his eyes wet with tears caused partly by the wind, partly by his misery and humiliation. But at the end of the two hours, he was rising to the trot; he had even cantered a few yards, and for a moment or two had known, for the first time, the joy of being at ease on horseback: feeling himself one with the horse, vitally aware of the balanced partnership of man and beast.

Riding home, Gerald dropped his instructor's manner as abruptly as he had assumed it, and became, as was his wont, suddenly jovial again. Duncan listened as though in a dream, hardly hearing a word, but aware of the friendly voice soothing his battered sensibilities like an incantation. His mind and body were lapped in a warm glow of triumph; rain set in before they reached the house, but nothing could have subdued that rich interior warmth. He felt, at that moment, happier than he had ever felt in his whole life.

In the hall, when they came in, Sims was perched on a step-ladder, hanging the mistletoe, which Gerald had collected that morning, from a hook in the ceiling.

Seeing it, Gerald chuckled.

"Pity the household doesn't run to some pretty girls," he said. Duncan laughed with him: the remark gave him a pleasing sense of being adult, of being able to share a "grown-up" joke with his uncle.

Gerald's eyes dropped to the boy's face, and the flushed, eager countenance roused in him a curious pang of regret: for the second time that day he found his mind dwelling, half-consciously, upon the idea of fatherhood. With a swift gesture, he drew Duncan towards him, and, leaning down, brushed his cheek with his lips.

Obscurely shocked by the sudden, unheralded contact, Duncan wriggled away. Gerald, himself rather embarrassed, subsided into a leather armchair with *The Times*. Once again, Duncan had the sense of crossing irrevocably some frontier into a country from which there could be no return.

At that moment Sims came in carrying a tea-tray. They drank their tea over the fire; Duncan still glowed with a sense of achievement and physical well-being. The foxes' masks, the football groups stared down approvingly upon his flushed face. His uncle, he thought, watching Gerald's huge body sprawled in the armchair, was of the race of heroes; and he felt rising within him, once again, a sense of passionate devotion to that cult of hardness which his new life had imposed upon him.

Soon after tea, Duncan wandered upstairs to his bedroom. Nothing had prepared him for the sudden sight of his mother's photograph, which stood on the window-ledge. Throwing himself on the bed, he burst into a passion of tears: sobbing as though his heart must break, for those green and innocent days in the West Country, the rounded and perfect world of his childhood, lost now beyond recall.

N EXT morning the bathroom-ritual was repeated; and Duncan found that the unaccustomed movements were beginning to come more easily to him. "Soon get you limbered up," Gerald prophesied.

The cold bath itself seemed less of an ordeal this morning; and in time, Duncan felt, he would even become accustomed to the noisy, naked presence of his uncle in the bathroom; already, on this, his second morning, it seemed less embarrassing.

"Hullo," Gerald exclaimed, as he picked up his razor. "Looks like a spot of blood. Funny — I could have sworn I cleaned it up yesterday. Perhaps Sims has been borrowing it?" He glared irritably at Duncan, who blushed, and pretended to be drying his face.

Back in his bedroom, Duncan dressed quickly, feeling a pleasant glow warming his body. Outside, the day was grey, with ragged, scudding clouds, and the brown woods crouched sullen and lifeless on the sky-line. He whistled as he dressed, feeling suddenly happy. From his trouser-pockets he took the cartridge-case and the rabbit-skull which he had picked up the day before, and placed them carefully on the window-sill, where he had already arranged his most treasured personal possessions: the photograph of his mother; a pressed specimen of a rare orchis, framed; a burnt-out rocket-case, souvenir of some long-past Guy Fawkes' night; *The Tale of Mr. Tod*, *The Coral Island*, and a brightly coloured picture-book, *Regiments of the British Army*.

Coming down to breakfast he found his uncle still at the table.

" 'Fraid I'll have to leave you alone today," he announced. "Got to go and see a chap over at Bladenwold. It's quite a longish run. Will you be able to amuse yourself? You can go round with Jarvis if you like — he's having a day with the rabbits. . . ." Gerald jerked his thumb at the bookcase as he went out: "Don't know if you're much of a reader. . . . Probably there's not much here in your line — sporting stuff, mostly. Help yourself, though, if you've nothing better to do."

DUNCAN carried out Gerald's advice to the letter, with the conscientious earnestness of a recruit performing some tedious but honourable fatigue. In the morning he went round with Jarvis, in the afternoon he read *Jorrocks*. The day passed pleasantly enough. Towards evening it began to rain. At six o'clock he had his supper alone. Gerald was not expected back until late. After supper he read *Jorrocks* again till nine o'clock. Then he went to bed, feeling the contented satisfaction of one who has performed his duties conscientiously.

Outside, a storm was rising. Duncan's bed was under the

window, and after the light was out he watched the new moon riding the ragged, rain-filled clouds. Later, curled up in bed, he lay awake luxuriously listening to the rising wind. At intervals, he could detect what seemed to be a passage of wild, unfamiliar music; perhaps it was pure imagination, or possibly Sims had switched on the wireless downstairs. . . . Presently he found himself upon the beaches of the Island, where he greeted his uncle without surprise, as an expected guest; even the fact that Gerald wore nothing but a pair of Aertex shorts and a singlet seemed normal and comprehensible. Sailing beyond the lagoon, in a small boat, they encountered a shark; Gerald, in an attempt to harpoon it, capsized the boat, and with Duncan on his back, reached the lagoon with five seconds to spare. . . . It must have been about midnight when Duncan was roused by Gerald's return. His uncle moved clumsily about the room, and once he dropped something and swore. Presently he opened the door softly and looked in.

"You asleep? Oh, you're not. Hope I didn't wake you." He stared into the half-darkness, as though he were trying to see Duncan more distinctly. His voice sounded furry, rather guttural. "Well, good night, old boy — sleep well," he muttered, and closed the door. Five minutes later Duncan could hear him snoring. For a little longer he lay listening to the wind whistling round the house. Then he turned over, and in a few minutes was peacefully asleep.

NEXT day was Christmas Eve, and dinner that night had already a semi-festive air. Duncan, still young enough to be impressed by "late dinner," was further confirmed in his adult status by being allowed a glass of claret and half a glass of port. Gerald had taken him riding again, and the wine completed his sense of glowing, physical well-being. He was in a mood to make the most of the occasion.

Gerald talked about horses; horses led to the war. The war led to India, polo, pig-sticking. Duncan was fascinated: partly by the reminiscences themselves, appropriate as they were to the heroic rôle for which he had cast his uncle; partly by the fact that himself had been chosen as their recipient. To Duncan, Gerald was already a hero: it was the merest accident that he had not been awarded the V.C. The stories of his athletic past helped to complete the picture; listening to his uncle's talk, Duncan was spell-bound, as he had been on the first morning, when Gerald took him round the farm. But the anecdotes of the war, of polo, Rugger-matches and the rest had a more potently magical quality, and, as they issued from Gerald's lips, were carefully stored away in the recesses of his mind whence, later, they would be disinterred to form part of the endless, episodic saga of the "Island," in which Gerald now invariably played the leading rôle.

In point of fact, Gerald was not in the least aware of conferring any honour by his random recollections. The truth was—

as he had half-realized on the day after Duncan's arrival — that he was badly in need of a companion or, rather, of an audience, and Duncan fulfilled this need perfectly. No grown-up would have listened to him with Duncan's blend of respect and intelligent interest. A man would have changed the subject, or contradicted him, or capped his anecdotes with others of his own; a woman would have pretended to listen for five minutes, and then uttered something totally irrelevant. But Duncan was the perfect listener; he drank in every word, and actually asked for more.

It was the first of many such evenings. On Christmas night, over the turkey and plum-pudding, Gerald unbent still further, and on succeeding nights it became a habit with him, when the port was on the table, to settle down to a further instalment of his autobiography. Duncan never seemed to tire of hearing about his athletic triumphs, or of the exploits of his battalion at the battle of the Somme. If his uncle appeared to be running dry, he would ask for some of the previous anecdotes over again, and Gerald was only too ready to oblige. Sometimes, by repetition, the stories acquired fresh details, or occasionally Gerald would give them an entirely new twist; unconsciously, he embroidered upon the bare facts, but except when he flagrantly contradicted himself — which was seldom — Duncan maintained a flattering attitude of complete credulity.

Sometimes, if Duncan were still awake when his uncle came to bed, the saga would continue in the bedroom. This Duncan particularly enjoyed; lying drowsily under the bed-clothes, with Gerald sprawled across the foot of the bed, the stories seemed to blend themselves almost instantaneously into the fabric of his Island-phantasy, so that the Island seemed suddenly to impinge upon reality, and the bedroom became the log-cabin, with savages and wild beasts prowling in the darkness beyond the window.

As the days passed, Duncan found himself growing more and more acclimatized to the new life. The riding-lessons continued — arduous, certainly, but never so exacting as that first, heroic ordeal. At first Gerald took him out every day; later, Sims or the groom became his companions — not so critical as his uncle, they made the daily rides more of a pleasure and less of an ordeal, and Duncan steadily improved. In his spare time, he worked in the derelict flower-garden, and sometimes found odd jobs for himself on the farm. Shortly after his first riding-lesson he was fitted for a pair of whipcord breeches of the same pattern as Gerald's; and he spent a considerable time admiring himself in them before the tall mirror in his uncle's bedroom. He began to be rather dissatisfied with his personal appearance, and next time he went to the barber's demanded an almost military crop, keeping what remained of his unruly hair carefully plastered down with Brylcreem. Undressing in the evenings, he would stand, again, naked before the mirror, staring critically at his body, flexing his muscles, fancying that he could detect, each day, an increase in their bulk. He was concerned, too, about what seemed to him the inadequate growth of hair on his body: he would have liked to be as hairy as his uncle. One morning — for he had grown less timid of late about physical matters — he mentioned the subject to Gerald himself, in the bathroom. Gerald was reassuring. "That'll come, like everything else," he said. "You're only thirteen, after all."

HIS fit of crying after that first riding-lesson had marked the final break with the old world. His nostalgia, if it recurred at all, was a rather stylized affair, a mere romantic melancholy, rather pleasant than otherwise. He found that he could now even look at his mother's portrait with no more than a conventional respect for the dead. The very fact that he could do so caused a slight stirring of guilt: it was as though he possessed two contrasted personalities, like two separate rooms, one of which he had deliberately chosen to inhabit, to the exclusion of the other. Yet the other room remained: he could glimpse it, as it were, through a half-open doorway, aware of his old preoccupations lingering round the walls, like pieces of half-forgotten furniture.

Standing idle for a moment in the garden or in his bedroom, he was sometimes aware of his old self, as he had perceived it in the train on his way to Priorsholt, hanging, as it were, in midair, outside his body: a composite image comprising a corner of the drawing-room at home, a vase of lilac and columbines, his mother's workbox, an old oil-painting of a wolf devouring a kid beneath a waning moon. But somehow the image had become dim, like a faded, rubbed-out picture in some old book. Smoothing his hair, or sliding his hand inside his shirt over the firm, warm flesh, he returned to the immediate awareness of his body; and before his eyes danced a procession of images far more vivid than any from the past, uncoordinated yet forming to some extent a comprehensible and logical whole: a rabbit-skull, a sprig of mistletoe, a streak of scarlet blood zigzagging across his uncle's bare chest.

ONE afternoon, when he was riding with Sims over the hills near the barracks, a file of soldiers, cross-country runners, passed by them: strung out loosely across the rising downland, running doggedly, in a morose silence. Their heavy limbs, protruding from skin-tight singlets and shorts, were stained and mottled with dull bluish-red by the sharp wind. Duncan remembered his first morning at Priorsholt, when the soldiers, in full marching-order, had passed the garden-gate. A curious feeling of satisfaction, almost a sense of fulfilment, possessed him as he realized that these naked runners — perhaps the same who had passed him that first morning — were no longer the strange fauna of an alien country, but co-habitants, comrades in a world to which himself now irrevocably belonged: a hard world, but no longer hostile, a soldier's land.

ON another afternoon, they took the path up through the woods to the field with the ancient stones.

It was towards the end of the holidays: a grey, windless day of mid-January, promising frost at night. A deep silence brooded over the woods, and as they approached the hurdle leading into the field, Sims, who had been rather talkative, fell silent too. At the wood's edge, a keeper had hung up a row of dead stoats and weasels. The field, as they passed into it, struck suddenly cold after the woods. A small, glacial wind rippled over the grasses, and Duncan noticed, without much curiosity, a fragment of white cloth or paper flapping from the twisted thornbush near the stones. He could hear, too — or fancied he could hear — a high, thin, singing noise, like the sound the wind makes in telegraph-wires. He looked round, but there were no wires in sight, except for a row of pylons which straddled across the valley some distance away, too far to be audible here.

"Queer sort of place," Sims remarked. "They calls it California — Lord knows why. See down in that valley? It's dry now. Well, ten to one, when you come back home in the spring, it'll be flooded. There's a stream rises farther up — they calls it the woe-water in these parts — they say when it rises, it brings trouble. One of those old wives' tales, I expect. It hasn't risen these last two years, so it's about due."

They cantered twice round the field, then turned their horses towards the path again. The field, screened by the silent, dead-seeming woods, appeared to Duncan like a room insulated by cork or rubber from the outside world. If one shouted one's loudest, he thought, there would be no echo, nobody beyond the wood's fringe would ever hear. An odd fancy possessed him, too, that if one came up here by oneself, one would never find the way back. It was stupid, of course: the path was obvious enough. Besides, he had been here by himself, the first day. . . . But then, he remembered, his uncle had ridden up just as he was starting back; so that proved nothing, after all. Suddenly he remembered the dead sheep, and glanced round, half-fearfully, to see if it was still there; but it seemed to have been removed.

A vague, unseizable depression descended on him. Then he remembered, suddenly, a children's party he had been to years ago, where they had played hide-and-seek. He had hidden behind a thick curtain, in a dark passage; to this day, he could remember the stifling, musty smell of the curtain. He had waited for what seemed hours, and at last heard the seeker approaching his hiding-place. He had stood there, scarcely daring to breathe, clenching his hands in an agony of terror: waiting for the sudden pounce in the dark. . . . The field, with its surrounding woods, produced in him a somewhat similar sensation. The sense of depression lasted almost till they reached the house, affecting him with a curious physical discomfort. He wondered, vaguely, if he were going to be ill.

At tea, however, his uncle was more than usually jovial, and in the fire-lapped comfort, listening to Gerald's cheerful, disconnected talk, Duncan was able to forget his earlier depression. Yet the sensation lingered in his mind, overtaking him unexpectedly at unoccupied moments; haunting his mind like an unpleasant echo.

G ERALD, shaving himself in the bathroom one morning, remembered that today was the last day of Duncan's holidays. The time seemed to have passed extraordinarily quickly; he realized, with some surprise, that he would miss the boy's companionship. "I'll have to find time to run down to the school," he thought.

At that moment Duncan entered the bathroom, his towel over his shoulder. In the last weeks he had almost entirely lost his modesty about stripping naked before Gerald, and now, without more ado, he slipped off his pyjama-jacket, and looked expectantly at Gerald; the morning exercises had become a ritual to miss which would have dislocated the whole day.

"By Jove, you look a darned sight fitter than when you came here," Gerald exclaimed. "You're getting some muscle on you, too." He grasped Duncan's arm, flexing the elbow with his other hand. "There's a big difference," he remarked, appreciatively. "You feel fitter, don't you?"

Duncan nodded.

"O.K., then—are you all set?" Gerald bent his arms to the "ready" position, and Duncan followed suit. The movements came far more easily to him nowadays, and he did, without doubt, feel a good deal fitter than at the beginning of the holidays.

"I'll be quite sorry when you've gone back," Gerald remarked, with a grin of rather disarming *naïveté*.

Duncan smiled back nervously; not for the world would he have betrayed the emotion which Gerald's words had suddenly roused in him. At that moment, had Gerald ordered him to jump, naked as he was, out of the window, he would have obeyed without a second thought. Since no such order was forthcoming, he turned away towards the bath, and plunged, with a passionate resolution, into the icy water.

LATE that afternoon, Gerald burst into the sitting-room, where Duncan was reading, with an excited and self-important air. He carried a large parcel, and a bundle of sticks about five feet long.

"Thought we'd have a bit of a do," he said. "Being your last night, you know. Undo 'em."

Duncan untied the parcel; infected by Gerald's excitement, his fingers trembled as he did so.

"Fireworks!" he exclaimed, delightedly.

"You like 'em, don't you?" Gerald said. "I remember you were talking about them once." Duncan remembered, too; one of Gerald's after-dinner stories had centred about some long-past firework-display, and the topic had kindled, in Duncan, memories of one of his own earlier "crazes." Gerald, evidently, had not failed to observe his interest. He had been generous, too: spreading out the fireworks on the table, Duncan realized that he must have spent several pounds. The variously shaped pieces, in their bright and starry paper wrappings, exercised a potent fascination over him; he examined them with a concentrated attention, reading the labels: Rockets with coloured stars, Italian streamers, Mines of Serpents, Devils-among-the-Tailors, Roman Candles — they were all there.

"I thought we might have a bit of a bonfire, too," Gerald was saying. "There's a hell of a lot of old junk up in the box-room. If you'll give us a hand to clear some of it out, we'll have a lovely blaze."

After tea they went up together to the box-room, an attic at the top of the house, which Duncan had not visited before. Gerald seemed oddly excited, almost more so than Duncan himself. The room was piled to the ceiling with cases, odd bits of furniture, picture-frames, unwanted ornaments. In one corner was a large wicker basket entirely filled with stuffed animals and birds: a stoat, a capercailzie, owls, squirrels, a pine-marten, and many others.

"They're the remains of the pater's museum — he was a bit of a collector. They're all moth-eaten, anyway. It's no earthly good keeping them. We'll cremate them. The basket's falling to bits, too. You can cart the lot down together."

Rather reluctantly, Duncan prepared to pick up the basket.

"Couldn't I keep one or two?" he asked. "I'd rather like this—" He pulled out the pine-marten.

"No." The peremptory note came into Gerald's voice.

"You'll only be getting moths in your clothes. Get rid of the lot of them. And while you're down there, get some wood out of the woodshed to start the fire. I'll sort out some of the rest of this junk while you're doing that."

Obediently, Duncan staggered downstairs with his curious burden. The bonfire was to be at the back of the house, on a rubbish-patch by the kitchen-garden. Dumping the basket he went to the woodshed, and carried out an armful of logs.

Gerald was already by the site, with a pile of straw and old cardboard boxes.

"That's the stuff. Pile 'em on. Pity to waste these oak-logs, actually — they're too good for a bonfire. Still, it doesn't matter. I got 'em when they cleared that patch up by California. . . . Right, let's go and get some more."

Back in the box-room, Duncan picked up a peculiar metal contraption from a shelf.

"What on earth's this?" he asked.

Gerald laughed.

"I'd forgotten about them. Haven't set eyes on 'em for years. . . . Don't you see what they are?"

"They look like handcuffs."

"They are. The pater brought them back from one of his trips — China, or somewhere. They're rather a curiosity. I forget the story about them. They're of no value, anyway."

Duncan looked at the heavy steel rings with sudden interest.

"Can I have them?" he asked, rather timidly.

Gerald stared at him, in surprise.

"Yes, take 'em if you want them. They're no good to me. Thinking of being a policeman, are you? Look out you don't get playing with them when you're by yourself, though. I did once, when I was a kid, and got stuck in the things for a couple of hours — there was nobody about to take 'em off. You see" — he took the handcuffs, pointing out the mechanism — "you can fix 'em on yourself, but somebody else has to take 'em off. Here, try." He clipped the cuffs over Duncan's wrists. "See? You're helpless. O.K., we'll release you." He laughed. "Or supposing I didn't, eh? Supposing I popped you on the bonfire, and held you up by your toes?"

Ten minutes later, the preparations were completed: the bonfire piled ready, the fireworks lashed to the fence, rockets planted in empty beer-bottles. It was a clear, frosty night, with no wind; the display promised to be a success. As they waited for Sims, who had gone to fetch paraffin to pour on the bonfire, Duncan had time to wonder at this sudden celebration. Christmas had passed with no more than the conventional festivities; now, suddenly, in mid-January, Gerald seemed to have been belatedly attacked by the holiday spirit. His manner, beneath his joviality, had an extraordinary intentness. He seemed almost over-anxious lest anything should go wrong.

Sims arrived, shortly, with the paraffin.

"Right — all ready?" Gerald struck a match, and touched off a rocket. It sailed high over the woods, bursting in a cluster of coloured stars. Others followed. A Bengal light flooded the garden with an aching green radiance, changed to crimson, then to blue. Roman candles fired their rubies and emeralds into the smoke-hung darkness, crackers leaped and spluttered about the paths. A rocket went sideways, and nearly hit the thatched roof of an outhouse. . . . At last the bonfire leapt into a sheet of flame. By its light uncle and nephew regarded one another, laughing, united suddenly in a shared, feverish excitement. Sims poured on more paraffin, and the fire blazed high again. Gerald suddenly gripped Duncan's hand, and they remained thus for some minutes, watching the leaping flames. Duncan could feel his uncle's tense excitement communicate itself to him, flowing like a current through their clenched fingers.

"Bet you wouldn't jump across it now," Gerald said. It was a safe bet: the flames roared high into the air from the heart of the fire.

"I bet *you* wouldn't," Duncan retorted.

"Wouldn't I?" Gerald laughed, his eyes gleaming at the challenge. "Just watch, then." He stepped back a few paces, took a running jump, and leapt straight through the fire, to reappear, a moment later, apparently untouched by the flames.

Duncan regarded him with astonishment: the feat had seemed almost supernatural. Dark with admiration, his eyes stared up at Gerald's massive body, looming in the flickering brightness at his side. Gerald met his eyes and laughed, sliding his hand through the boy's arm, and rocking him gently backwards and forwards. The bonfire began to subside. Only the oak boughs remained now, and the wire skeleton of the wicker basket, in which the remains of the stuffed birds and animals were already unrecognizable. Gerald had stopped laughing. He was staring intently into the fire, as though his eyes perceived something beyond the charred débris, some vision vouchsafed to himself alone. He gripped Duncan's arm tightly, and again the boy felt the current of some deep emotion pass from the man's body to his own. The whole occasion seemed to have a peculiar ritual significance, as though the bonfire and the fireworks were a ceremony performed especially in the boy's honour. Puzzled, he felt a certain relief when Sims' voice broke across the silence.

"You've forgotten the big rocket, sir."

Duncan felt his uncle's grip relax.

"Oh, yes — the big rocket." Gerald sounded suddenly tired, and bored with the whole affair. Casually, he struck a match, held it to the touch-paper, and stepped backwards out of the way. There was a hissing roar of flame, and the rocket soared magnificently into the night, arching away over the woods, and bursting at last in a dazzling shower of silver and golden rain.

"That's travelled some distance," Sims remarked. "Shouldn't wonder if it hadn't dropped right over in the valley, beyond California."

"I shouldn't wonder," Gerald agreed. He looked at his watch. "Come on," he said to Duncan, "it's past dinner-time."

Duncan picked up the handcuffs, which he had put in a safe place on the path, and followed Gerald reluctantly into the house. The moment had a poignant finality: the fireworks were over, and so were the holidays—tomorrow he returned to school. And he felt, too obscurely, that the occasion marked the end of something more important than either: it was as though he had crossed, irrevocably, yet another boundary, separating him still more completely from the innocent, half-forgotten world of his childhood.

THE next day dawned with rain, a steady hopeless downpour, blotting out the countryside, making it anonymous: no longer the place that Duncan had learnt to know, but a mere point on the ordnance map. The veil of mist and rain, by concealing the familiar landmarks, softened the ache of departure; to Duncan the last few weeks seemed already unreal, half-merged in phantasy. In the garden, the charred remains of the fireworks lay scattered over the paths and beds: mute souvenirs of a ritual which had once seemed immensely important. Leaving the house, the boy felt a sudden sense of disintegration: connections snapped in his mind, things seemed to be falling apart. Owing to the mist, no doubt, the house and garden seemed smaller and rather squalid; even Gerald himself seemed in some way diminished. He talked cheerfully, as they drove into Glamber, of next holidays: as though the four weeks in the spring would be a mere repetition, in no way different from the weeks just past. Duncan, knowing otherwise, found his uncle's assumption irritating; things never did, as he well knew, turn out the same, or happen as one expected them to. The last month seemed to him already sealed off from the present and future: a pocket existing outside time, a small and perfect world never to be revisited.

IN the afternoon, after seeing his nephew off from Glamber, Gerald strolled aimlessly out of the house, and took the path up through the woods. He seldom walked for the sake of walking; but today the house and farm had become suddenly oppressive.

The mist had cleared slightly, and trees and undergrowth dripped with a heavy moisture. No sound disturbed the drenched wintry stillness. At the top of the path, the stoats and weasels still hung gibbeted from the wire. Out in the field, the stones rose dimly in the misty air. On the thornbush nearby, something white fluttered indistinctly.

It was a depressing place, Gerald thought, wondering why he had come. He remembered how, the morning after Duncan's arrival, he had ridden up the path and jumped the hurdle, nearly landing on top of the boy. A vaguely unpleasant memory flashed through his mind, half-formulated, elusive: Duncan's face, crestfallen, questioning, half-frightened. What had happened to make him look like that? Irrelevantly, Gerald found himself wondering what sort of time the boy had at school; he had never said much about it. The subject lingered in his mind, irritatingly; the fact that Duncan was not there to talk about it seemed disproportionately annoying. He would miss the boy a lot, he realized; the evenings, in particular, would be lonely. Duncan, he thought, was shaping well, considering his disadvantages. He had learnt to ride, and he looked twice as fit as he'd looked at the beginning of the holidays. One couldn't do much more for the kid, Gerald reflected. Yet beneath his regret at Duncan's departure, there was a curious sense of relief: it was as though the weight of some responsibility had been suddenly lifted from him.

Turning on his heel, he started back abruptly down the path, lashing at the undergrowth with his riding-crop.

The prospect of a lonely dinner that night unnerved him. On a sudden impulse, he got out the car and drove over to a large pleasure-town some way along the coast, where he was not well known. He dined, expensively, at a hotel, and afterwards drank heavily in the bar. Returning at midnight, he listened to a late news-bulletin on the wireless. It looked as though there were almost certain to be war, and the prospect evoked in him a queer excitement; some nerve in him responded with an extraordinary sensitiveness to the idea of fighting and destruction. He was filled, suddenly, with an immense exultation—as though he were a condemned prisoner who hears a rumour of reprieve.

PART TWO

The Sacrifice

TOWARDS the end of the term Duncan was expelled from school. A series of petty thefts had occurred in his house, over a period of weeks, and were traced, eventually, to Duncan, who, for that matter, was a bad criminal and had not made any very serious efforts at concealment.

His thieving at first seemed quite motiveless: some flint arrow-heads from the school-museum, a bicycle-chain, a skipping-rope, a pair of football boots, a leather belt — all these disappeared, and all were found in his possession. None of the stolen articles was of much value; when asked by he had taken them, Duncan could only reply that he had "liked them rather." The housemaster, puzzled, was at first inclined to take a lenient view; he had a talk to the boy, maintaining a friendly attitude throughout, but pointing out the gravity of the offence, and warning him that any repetition of it would have to be dealt with severely. A week later a pair of football-shorts disappeared from the changing-room; this also was traced to Duncan who, for the first time in his life, was caned. A few days later, some sweets and a bottle of hair-oil were taken from a boy's locker, and a packet of cigarettes belonging to one of the masters. The case was put before the head-master, and Duncan was formally expelled.

The head-master wrote sensibly, even sympathetically, to Gerald. It had seemed at first a mere case of kleptomania, he said; boys of Duncan's age did sometimes go through such a phase; but the later thefts had seemed to point in another direction. The boy appeared to be incorrigible, and had adopted an attitude of sullen defiance throughout. He seemed quite impenitent, even now. The head-master went on to express his regrets, etc.; a promising boy in many ways, but Gerald would understand that one had to consider his "influence" upon the house. Doubtless he would fare better at some school which made a specialty of such "difficult" cases.

After his first shocked surprise, Gerald adopted what he honestly believed to be a just and temperate attitude to the affair. He tried to consider, impartially, what was best to be done. The head-master's suggestion of "special" schools he rejected — psychology and all that was nonsense, so far as he was concerned. On the other hand, no decent school would take the boy at present. One would have to make careful inquiries. Meanwhile, it seemed a case for strict discipline; one didn't want to be harsh, but what the boy obviously needed was a regular routine with a fixed scale of punishments. Pity he was too young to start thinking about the Army, Gerald reflected. He had a genuine faith in Army methods applied to such a case as

Duncan's; the least he could do was to try to provide an efficient substitute.

The whole business was, of course, a damned nuisance. He remembered his unwillingness to have the boy in the first place, his feeling that the whole thing was a mistake. Well, events had proved his fears justified — though even he had not expected things to turn out quite so badly. God knew, he had enough worries, without this; the farm seemed under a curse — nothing seemed to go right. A plantation of young fruit-trees, Gerald's particular hope and pride, had been attacked by some rare and insidious disease. There was foot-and-mouth in the neighbourhood, too. The foxes were getting too many chickens. And the wheat looked poorer than for two years past. And now Duncan was returning before he was due, returning in disgrace; and likely, Gerald thought, to remain for some time, unless a decent school could be found to take him.

The head-master's letter arrived in the morning; Duncan was to arrive the same afternoon. Waiting for him, once again, on the draughty station at Glamber, Gerald was aware that, in spite of the circumstances, he was glad to get him back. The past two months had dragged by interminably. By day, he had thrown himself into the work of the farm with renewed energy, though without any renewed interest: it was a question, merely, of his livelihood. At night, dog-tired, yet unable to face the lonely evenings, he took to paying calls in the neighbourhood (unwelcome, most of them, for Gerald's popularity was not increasing), or else he drove over to the neighbouring towns. He was drinking more nowadays than ever before, and he was less able to afford it. Once or twice he went to London, for weekends; he had intended visiting Duncan at the school, but the plan, for one reason or another, had come to nothing.

When the boy stepped out of the train, Gerald immediately recognized a change in him: the last vestiges of his childhood had left him, and he had that air of precocious, spurious sophistication which some boys of his age acquire, usually for no good reason, and which seems, too often, to retard their normal development, lasting sometimes well into manhood. Duncan looked smart, defiant, and rather unhealthy.

Gerald greeted him with little more than his usual abruptness. Duncan was polite, and apparently quite unmoved. They drove through the bright March evening in silence. An equinoctial gale, which had raged for the last three days, was gradually blowing itself out. Violent gusts of wind swept the countryside intermittently, succeeded by intervals of calm. The sky looked immensely clear and clean, as though it had been washed. Ragged clouds raced along the horizon, and the distant woods heaved and rippled in the brief, irregular bursts of wind.

Back at Priorsholt, Gerald followed Duncan up to his room. Once there, the boy's self-possession seemed to fall away from him; he looked frightened and pathetic, and Gerald felt his good intentions weakening.

"Now then," he began. "Just tell me what all this is about. What made you do these things?"

Duncan stared back at him without expression.

"I don't know," he said.

"But look here; you know it's wrong to take what doesn't belong to you. You've never done it before — at least, not since I've known you. What made you start?"

"I don't know." Duncan's face was still wooden.

"But you must have *some* idea. You knew those things belonged to other people — or belonged to the school. What made you take them?"

"I don't know. . . ." Seeing his uncle wince, impatiently, at the repetition, Duncan added, "I suppose I wanted them, sort of."

"You *suppose* you wanted them?" Gerald's voice was impatient, and he spoke more harshly. "Well, see here, my lad; I don't know if you realize it, but you've landed yourself in a nasty mess. You've been expelled for theft; it's bad enough in itself. What you probably don't know is that no other school — no decent one — will feel inclined to take you. And that's not all; a chap that's expelled from a public school — expelled for dishonesty — stands a rather poor chance of making good in after life. You're young, I know; I don't for a moment think you're a confirmed criminal. I'll even go so far as to say that I think the school's been a bit hasty. At the same time no school can afford to keep a thief. That's the point, you see."

His words, he thought, had made some impression. Duncan looked frightened, and inclined to cry.

"Now listen," Gerald went on. "In the first place, we've got to think out what's best for you. You've got to be educated somewhere, presumably, but no school 'll take you after this, unless it's some second-rate place, or one of those queer schools, co-educational and all that. I'll have to think about it. Meanwhile, you probably haven't thought how difficult it's going to be for me. . . . It's a nice thing, when people ask how you're doing, to have to say, 'Oh, the boy's been expelled from school, for theft. . . .' I'll have to give it out that you've come home for health-reasons or something. . . . Meanwhile" — Gerald's voice took on a firmer tone — "meanwhile you've got to pull yourself together. You can no doubt get on with some of your school-work for the time being; I'll do my best to help you. I shall also see that you're given some regular work on the farm. Otherwise I don't propose to punish you any further."

Duncan's face expressed something like relief. Gerald, how-ever, unwilling that he should suppose himself forgiven so easily, frowned discouragingly.

"But you'd better get this quite clear from the start," he re-sumed. "I want your solemn promise that you won't — that all this business is going to stop. Now, will you promise me?"

"Yes," said Duncan easily, without appearing particularly impressed.

"Do you faithfully promise — word of honour?"

"Yes, on my word of honour."

Gerald looked dissatisfied.

"And understand," he added, "the first time I catch you doing or saying anything in the least dishonest — you're for it. I shall have no alternative but to give you a damned good thrashing. Is that quite clear?"

Duncan nodded.

"That's all, then." Gerald left him, feeling that the interview had been inconclusive, almost meaningless. Duncan had been naturally a bit scared — but that was all. No signs of being really repentant, or of having formed any genuine resolution. He had seemed to be only half-listening, most of the time: his eyes had stared back, frightened, and (though Gerald tried to disregard this) with a look of inarticulate pleading.

Downstairs, Gerald's eye fell on a calendar. The twenty-fifth of March. . . . Suddenly he remembered that today was Duncan's birthday.

"Poor little brat," he thought. "It's bad luck on him."

LEFT alone, Duncan began to unpack, mechanically laying out his treasures on the window-ledge: the photograph, the orchis, the skull, the handcuffs. . . . He cried a little, from fatigue and the nervous strain of the past days. Presently he knelt up on the bed and leaned out of the window. The woods were bloomed with purple buds, and here and there showed a patch of young, tender green. By the pathway, leading up the hill, the yews and hollies stood out dark, impenetrable, against the clear, cold western sky. From the garden came an evening chorus of bird-song, mingled with the thin bleating of lambs from the nearby fields, and another sound, monotonous, indistinct — perhaps a wireless-set in some cottage, or merely the wind itself. Sims crossed the garden, carrying a bucket; a dog barked, and from the stables came the muffled noises of the horses. Duncan perceived the familiar landmarks, but they seemed to have no meaning: recognizable, but unreal, like a photograph. As he watched, the light drained out of the sky and the far fields, and the brown shaggy-crested woods seemed to creep nearer: watchful, possessive, but without pity.

NEXT day the new régime began. Duncan spent the morning in his room with his school-books, pretending to do arithmetic, which happened to be the subject at which Gerald felt safest. In the afternoon he was given a job with one of the farm-hands—hoeing. In his encounters with Gerald he was polite and self-effacing. As much as possible Gerald avoided him, and after dinner that night pretended that he had work in his office.

Something, Gerald decided, would have to be done; at dinner the constraint had been unbearable — both of them remembered last holidays, the glasses of port, the reminiscences. It would be easy enough to slip back into the old intimacy, and Gerald was half-tempted to do so; then he remembered that his nephew was a thief, and had been expelled from school. The fact seemed incredible: looking at Duncan, he wondered if the boy was really mentally ill. It didn't seem likely; Duncan was normal enough in every other respect. In which case, of course, there was no excuse for his dishonesty; and this being so, he must be shown that he couldn't just take up his life at home again where he had left it off. Gerald, rather reluctantly, hardened his heart: the boy must be taught a lesson, once and for all.

Sitting in his "office," he went over the farm-accounts for the fiftieth time; there was no doubt about it, the place was being run at a loss. He had done his damnedest; but it seemed, now, that no amount of ungrudged labour could make up for the lack of necessary capital. Capital! Where was he to get it? Briefly, unhopefully, he ran over the diminishing list of former friends whom he might approach. . . . But there was nobody — nobody who would be prepared, on the score of past friend-ship, to sink money in a failing concern.

That very morning Gerald had made a tour of the farm and buildings, attempting roughly to assess the amount he would require to set the place on its feet. The lowest, most conserva-tive estimate seemed beyond the bounds of reasonable hope. Not only the land itself and the farm-buildings needed money spent upon them: the very house itself was falling into decay. Had it been a labourer's cottage, it would have been con-demned by now. . . . Walls needed repointing, windows sagged on their hinges; the roof leaked — on more than one occasion lately Sims, who slept at the top of the house, had been swamped out. For years, Gerald had postponed repairs, waiting till he should have "turned the corner" financially; but the cor-ner was yet unturned, and meanwhile, in the spring rains, the house was becoming less and less weatherproof. It was not merely his financial position which was threatened now; soon, unless he took drastic action, he would be deprived of the most elementary physical comforts—a roof over his head and a dry bed.

Crouching over the books in the chilly room, he could hear the wind rising yet again, and rattling the loose windows; rain spattered dismally on the uncurtained panes. He had a curious sense of being beleaguered: the elements themselves were hostile, the whole world seemed against him.

He longed to rejoin his nephew in the sitting-room; to offer him a glass of port, to slip back into their old, easy companionship. He resisted the temptation, however, and tried, once again, to concentrate on the figures before him. Later, he switched on the news. If war came, he thought, it would at least be a solution to his own problems. He would sell up the farm for what he could get, or the Government would take it over. Once again, the prospect of war filled him with an obscure, rather shameful excitement. Things certainly sounded pretty bad: there seemed every likelihood that the country would be at war before the autumn.

Presently he heard his nephew going up to bed, and returned to the sitting-room. He poured out a stiff whisky and sod and prepared himself for the lonely evening ahead.

THE following day was spent by Duncan in a similar manner, except that in the afternoon he went out for a short ride with Sims. The servant suspected something irregular about his return, but tact made him silent, and the ride was a rather depressing business. They rode up through the woods, coming out into the field called California by a different path, so that the sight of the stones took Duncan by surprise. The fact, too, that the valley below the field was almost under water made the landscape unfamiliar.

Sims, seeing him looking down at the flooded fields, spoke for the first time for several minutes.

"Yes, the old river's up. I told you it would be, d'you remember?"

Duncan remembered: and remembered, too, that it was the woe-water, the bringer of trouble. Another memory recurred, and he looked round, almost without thinking, for the dead sheep: unreasonably, since he knew it had been removed before the end of the holidays. A black object under a thorn-bush roused his curiosity. It proved, on examination, to be a dead rook.

"Don't touch it," Sims advised (for Duncan had dismounted to look at it), "they say they carry diphtheria."

They rode home almost in silence; the late afternoon sunlight slanted between the thickets, gleaming wine-coloured on the dogwood saplings, touching with sudden brilliance the young green of the hazels. Primroses starred the path's edge, and the first paper-thin anemones trembled in the thickets. For the first time since he returned, Duncan felt a flicker of interest in something outside himself, the revival of a long-forgotten pleasure. His mother had taught him to like wild-flowers, and for a time he had devoted himself, with one of his obsessional bursts of enthusiasm, to the collection of a herbarium. He wondered, now, if there were any rarities to be found in these parts.

After dinner that night, Gerald remained in the dining-room, but apart from a few unimportant remarks, he did not talk. Nor did he offer Duncan any wine, though he drank a considerable amount himself. Duncan pretended to read an old bound volume of *Punch*. At half-past eight, he excused himself and went to bed.

He felt immensely fatigued, but with a taut, strained weariness that prevented him from sleeping. Intermittently, a series of nervous spasms twitched his limbs, and occasionally he was surprised to find himself, quite unconsciously, lying completely rigid, as though expecting a blow. He lay with open eyes, starting into the darkness; for some weeks now, he had slept badly, troubled by an unreasonable anxiety, a sense of interminable waiting for he knew not what. Later in the evening, he heard his uncle come up to bed, but sleep was as far from him as ever. At one moment he felt an overmastering desire to escape from the house — to dress and go out, anywhere, into the woods, up to California. . . . Leaning out of the window, he listened to the night-noises — a pheasant disturbed by some animal, a dog barking, the faint whistle of a distant train.

Idly he fingered the rabbit skull, the handcuffs. Very vaguely, with a spasmodic groping after the truth, he tried to analyse what had happened to him since last holidays. Something had happened to change his world out of all knowledge; he remembered the last night before his return to school: the fireworks, Gerald laughing in the bonfire's blaze, the big rocket; and then the rainy morning, the desolate burnt-out cases strewing the garden, the departure. . . . His uncle had spoken cheerfully of "next holidays," but he had known, at the time, that things would be different. Dimly he remembered his sense of crossing some final boundary-line into an unknown world: and realized, half-consciously, that his present state was a logical outcome of that irrevocable act. It was then, he thought, that he had begun to have the sensation of "waiting." What he was waiting for, he didn't know; only, from time to time, the sense of danger recurred — that feeling of some vague, impending disaster which had haunted his first days at Priorsholt; reminding him of that long-distant children's party — the alcove in the dark corridor, the musty smell of the curtain, the footsteps moving furtively in the darkness.

For the first weeks at school, after returning from Priorsholt, he had lapsed into a chronic boredom: accepting the life of the school at its face value, doing his best at games, not exactly unhappy, but feeling — after that night of the bonfire and fireworks — as though virtue had gone out of him; and waiting, with a morose impatience, for some event, no matter what, which should restore some meaning to his existence.

The thefts were really a kind of game: an antidote to boredom, more than anything else. He didn't want the things, he would have given them back willingly, once taken; and he still found it in some way incomprehensible that acts which, to himself, seemed mere practical jokes, forgotten as soon as performed, should appear to others as crimes of the utmost gravity. In the first instance, there had been no calculated "dishonesty" about his thefts: the dishonesty had come afterwards, when he realized the grave view taken by authority. What had been a mere private joke became, at this later stage, a joke deliberately directed against the school. His earlier acquisitions—the flint arrow-heads, the bicycle-chain, and so on—had appealed to him in precisely the same way as the skull, the cartridge-case, the handcuffs on the window-ledge; the affair of the hair-oil and the cigarettes had been another matter: a conscious gesture of defiance against an authority which he hated and despised. Rather indiscreetly he had actually used the hair-oil (a fact which, among others, led to his discovery), and the cigarettes he had taken to a remote corner of the grounds and smoked, feeling rather sick: remembering the soldier in the train, the dark, weathered face and the faint reek of sweat.

Outside the window, the restless equinoctial wind began to rise again, striking cold through his thin poplin pyjamas. He remained at the window, letting the cold air penetrate his body, playing with the idea that he might catch pneumonia. Even to be ill, he thought, would make a change, would give back some kind of meaning to his existence.

Before any serious risk was run, however, he had crept back

to bed. He sank, at last, into a drowsy state in which phantasy merged imperceptibly into dream. On the "Island" a curious episode occurred: he found himself lashed to a tree-trunk, awaiting the assault of savages — a constantly recurring theme in the island-saga. Presently, from the woods round about, a number of figures converged upon the tree to which he was tied. They were indistinct, dressed in long robes of some kind: one of them, taller than the rest, appeared to be their leader. Their faces were invisible, concealed by white head-dresses like those of Arabs. Suddenly, one after another, the figures began to remove their hoods: each in turn exhibiting, instead of a human face, the red, bristling mask of a fox. Last of all, the leader uncovered himself, revealing the heavy, frowning countenance of Gerald March.

D URING the next few days there was a gradual relaxation of Gerald's disciplinary measures; not through any conscious change in his intentions, but merely because he lacked the time to be constantly supervising the boy's activities. Truth to tell, he was glad of the excuse to leave Duncan to his own devices, for his nephew's presence rather embarrassed him; moreover, Gerald was, in some respects, extremely lazy.

In the mornings, Duncan continued to make a pretence of working at his school-tasks, overlooked inadequately and at irregular intervals by his uncle. In the afternoons, however, he found it easy enough to avoid the jobs which Gerald had rather half-heartedly ordered. If Sims or the groom were free, they went riding; on the days when nobody was free to accompany him, he took to going for long walks by himself, in search of botanical rarities. With the advancing spring, his taste for plant-hunting had revived, and he had even unpacked an old flora by Anne Pratt which had belonged to his mother. The names of certain plants which he had never found haunted his imagination: moonwort, stinking hellebore, spider orchis, rampions, baneberry. The possibility of finding some of them provided an object for his walks. On one occasion, at least, his search was rewarded.

One day, rather late in the afternoon, he set out for the woods. The weather, fine for the last few days, showed signs of breaking-up again: a bank of cloud hung ominously over the woods, and the wind had moved round to the south-west. Duncan walked leisurely up the woodland path; at one point he noticed a narrow track on the right-hand side, which he did not remember, and he decided to explore it. The new path led on indeterminately, curving now to the right, now to the left, narrowing slightly as it progressed. Coming up the main path, the woodland had been noisy with birds; here it was perfectly silent. Duncan walked softly, the feeling of mystery, which haunts all woods, accentuating his own sense of irrational expectancy. Presently he came to a clearing; here the ground sloped abruptly to the right, and the path which he had been following took a sharp curve in the opposite direction. The slope was clothed with tall beech-trees, and the ground beneath them was thick with last year's leaves. There was little undergrowth — only a few bushes of spurge-laurel and the dark, holly-like clumps of butcher's-broom. Suddenly Duncan started forward: farther down the slope a tall plant had caught his attention — a high cluster of pale-green blossom surmounting a tuft of darker foliage. It might be a large plant of wood-spurge, but it seemed too robust; he hurried down the slope, and examined it briefly. There was no doubt about it, it was the stinking hellebore: one of the flowers he had always wanted to find. It was larger than he had expected from the pictures: an august and rather sinister-looking plant. The unopened buds drooped stiffly, bluntly pointed, like the heads of adders poised to strike; the expanded green flowers were fringed with a line of dull, thunderous purple. Nearby he saw another plant, and another . . . In the beechen dimness he could see the pale, drooping clusters receding, innumerable, between the silvery boles. He ran hither and thither, assuring himself that it was really the plant he thought. No doubt of it. . . . He felt strangely excited. Something had happened at last. . . . He gathered a bunch, and at length decided that it must be time to go home. He clambered up the slope again, making his way back, as he thought, by the same path. Soon, however, something about the track struck him as unfamiliar. A curious, cup-shaped fungus protruded from the trees, which themselves had changed, being mostly elder and ash instead of hazel. He noticed, too, some blotched, silvery orchis-leaves by the path's edge, which he had not seen before. Moreover, the path twisted continuously, and seemed to be going downhill. He retraced his steps, but the path forked several times, and at last he realized that he was lost.

He wandered on, rather hopelessly, losing all sense of direction, and taking any path at random. The sun was low, now, and he noticed that the clouds had swept up to the zenith. Presently it began to rain. He quickened his pace; the clouds had hastened the coming dusk, and he began to feel frightened. The wood was large, he knew, and even if he succeeded in getting out of it, he might find himself far from home. He hurried on: the paths all seemed alike, sometimes wider, sometimes narrower. He wished he could find the beech-hanger again, where he had found the hellebore, but he must have travelled a considerable distance since he left it. The darkness increased rapidly, and the rain became heavier. Drops from the trees spattered on his bare head, and down his open-necked shirt on to his chest; his body was hot from walking, and the rain struck unnaturally cold, like a physical manifestation of his fear. At last he stopped dead in his tracks, a helpless anxiety paralysing his limbs. A sudden sickening excitement crept over him, such as he had sometimes felt in dreams: a compulsive abandonment to something evil and perilous, which was half-agony, half-pleasure. The moment passed, leaving its physical tokens: he felt, all at once, emptied of all life, hopelessly weary; yet his mind had become curiously lucid. He struck along another path with renewed confidence, and found himself in the field of the stones, close to the tumuli. Passing the three ivy-covered mounds, he made for the hurdle, and paused, leaning against it, getting his breath. He was unbearably hot: his shirt clung to his body, drenched with rain and sweat. Unbuttoning it, he allowed the rain to fall unhindered on to his bare chest, breathing deeply, trying to still the trembling which shook his body.

At last, wet to the skin, he began to shiver in good earnest from the cold. By now it was almost dark; across the valley, a band of fading, yellowish light glowed dully between the scudding rain-clouds. Duncan felt a wave of misery sweep over him: a desolate unhappiness such as he had never experienced before. He would have liked to die: here, in this "bad place," among the stifling, malevolent woods. Like the sheep which he had seen, he would lie out on the grass for days and weeks, till the white, fleshy maggots swarmed in his belly. . . . Wave after wave of desolation broke over him, the vision of his own destruction printing itself, with an indelible horror, upon his mind. The bunch of hellebore hung limply, still, from his hand. Leaning against the hurdle, in the thickening darkness, scarcely aware of the drenching rain which beat across the field, he gave way to a passion of hysterical weeping.

AT dinner-time Duncan was still out, and Gerald began to feel anxious about him. Neither Sims nor anybody else had seen him since tea-time. Probably, thought Gerald, he was sheltering from the rain at some cottage, or he might be somewhere on the farm. Irritated, slightly apprehensive, he put on boots and a mackintosh, and, shoving an electric-torch into his pocket, plunged out into the night.

Squelching through the mud, he made a tour of the farm, calling Duncan's name, but without result. Telling Sims to keep a look-out, he walked out of the garden-gate, and he took the path up the hillside. It was a shot in the dark; but he had seen Duncan wandering off in that direction several times lately.

He walked quickly, almost running. Coming to the edge of the wood, he continued straight on, beneath the dripping trees. Occasionally he called Duncan's name: aware that the search was rather a futile proceeding — probably the boy was safely home by now.

He turned a corner; and came suddenly to the opening into the field. Bent over the hurdle, exhausted with misery and terror, Duncan did not realize his presence till Gerald spoke.

"What the devil have you been up to?" he exploded. Flashing his torch on the boy's face, he was startled by its appearance: pale as death, the eyes red with crying, the red hair tousled from the wind and rain. Gerald's voice, and the flash of the torch, made him flinch back, suddenly, with a motion of terror.

"What's up?" Gerald insisted.

"Nothing."

"Nothing! Why, you're drenched to the skin, you've been crying, you look — as if you'd seen a ghost. Why didn't you come back? What happened?"

Duncan looked at him, miserably, with a faintly-wondering air.

"I don't know," he said.

"I don't know." Gerald suddenly remembered the obstinate

phrase repeated, persistently, on the night of his arrival. "I don't know." A curious and disturbing idea occurred to Gerald; perhaps the boy was speaking the exact and literal truth; perhaps he honestly "didn't know."

Gerald felt a spasm of fear—fear of something unknown and unknowable against which he felt powerless.

"Well, come on home, for God's sake," he exclaimed. "You don't want to get pneumonia."

He opened his mackintosh, and pulled Duncan under its shelter. It was a capacious garment, big enough to cover the two of them. He hurried the boy down the path, pressing him closely to his side. Duncan's body was racked with a violent trembling, which had scarcely subsided when they reached the house.

Indoors, Gerald was shocked, afresh, by his appearance. He rang for Sims.

"Run a hot bath," he ordered. "Quick as you can. And bring down some towels and a dressing-gown."

He poured out a tot of whisky, and handed it to the boy.

"Get that down you," he ordered. "It'll keep the cold out."

Duncan obeyed. The spirit seemed like fire in his throat, and he began to cough. Suddenly Gerald noticed the bunch of hellebore, which Duncan still clutched in his hand.

"What's that you've got?" he asked, curiosity overcoming, for the moment, his concern for the boy's condition.

"Stinking hellebore," Duncan replied, mechanically.

"Stinking how-much? . . . Well, never mind that now — let's get those wet clothes off."

Sims had returned with the towels; before the blazing fire, Duncan allowed his uncle to strip off his drenched clothes and rub him down. Gerald worked efficiently, with an intense, silent concentration of purpose. When the boy's body glowed pink all over, and the colour had returned to his face, he handed him his pyjamas and dressing-gown.

"Is that bath ready?" Gerald asked Sims, who had remained in attendance.

"Yes, sir. But the roof's leaking, sir."

"Where? Which roof?"

"In Master Duncan's room, sir. Coming in in two places, it is. One over the bed, sir, and another by the door. It's drenched the top of the bed, sir."

The wind had risen to hurricane force; the house seemed to rock and tremble about them as they stood there, in apparent security, before the fire. Once again, Gerald had the feeling of being besieged: the enemy creeping nearer, the first artillery-fire opening up already.

"It would happen just this night of nights," he muttered. "Christ, what a damned nuisance. It's that penthouse roof — no protection. Have you moved the bed?"

"Yes, sir, but the room ain't hardly fit to sleep in."

"There's nowhere else," Gerald snapped, furious at what he

fancied was a note of reproof in Sims's voice: Sims had suffered himself from the leakages, and had, moreover, pointed out the state of the roof as far back as the summer.

Gerald turned to Duncan, who was crouched before the fire, his upward glance moving questioningly between the two men.

"You'd better nip upstairs and get into the bath," he said. "I'll come up and have a dekko."

Preceded by Duncan, Gerald made his way upstairs, followed by Sims.

"Have a good soak, and then give yourself a sharp rub-down again," Gerald advised, as Duncan disappeared into the bathroom.

The boy's bedroom was, as Sims had said, unfit to sleep in. Two large, spreading patches of wetness glistened on the ceiling: the water dripped in a continuous stream into the buckets which Sims had placed on the floor beneath. The head of the bed, which had been shifted out of range, was drenched through to the mattress.

"We'll have to make up another bed somewhere," Gerald muttered vaguely.

"Yes, sir," Sims agreed, and paused doubtfully, looking questioningly at his master. "Where would you suggest, sir?"

Still suspicious of Sims's attitude, Gerald turned upon him irritably.

"Oh, anywhere ——"

"Yes, sir."

Gerald thought quickly. No other upstairs room was habitable: on the rare occasions when he had had friends to stay, Gerald had accommodated them in the small room which Duncan had lately occupied.

"He'd better sleep in my bed for tonight. . . . I'll get on to the builder-people first thing in the morning. . . . Better fix him up with a hot-water bottle — have we got one? And give him a hot drink in bed — and some food if he wants it. He'll be in for a nasty chill if we don't look after him. . . . Can't think what he was up to — out in all that weather."

Silent, and still (Gerald felt) critical, Sims retired. Gerald lingered in the bedroom, listening to the clamour of the wind, until he heard Duncan's bath-water running away. Then he walked across to the bathroom.

Duncan was climbing into his pyjamas. His colour was normal now, his eyes brighter — though he still, Gerald thought, looked as if he'd seen a ghost.

"Whatever possessed you to stay out in all that storm?" Gerald asked, bluffly.

Duncan stared at him with a nervous intentness. The inevitable reply rose to his lips.

"I don't know," he muttered.

"But you must know. Did you meet somebody, did something scare you?" Gerald insisted.

Duncan shook his head. He could give no satisfactory explanation, persist as Gerald might in his questioning. He had got

lost, he admitted; it had got dark and begun to rain, and he had
felt frightened.

"But you knew where you were when I found you — why ever
didn't you come home?"

"I don't know," the boy replied.

"Well," said Gerald briskly, "your room's uninhabitable, so
you'd better tuck up in my bed for tonight. Sims is bringing
you a drink. . . . Try and get to sleep. I'll ask Sims if he's got an
aspirin."

At length, having seen Duncan comfortably installed in the
big double-bed, Gerald went downstairs to dinner. Before the
meal, he drank several glasses of sherry rather quickly; with the
meal he drank claret; and afterwards asked Sims to open a new
bottle of port.

He sat for a long time, drinking, over the fire, listening to
the roar of the wind and the angry gusts of rain beating against
the windows. A sense of hopelessness, against which alcohol
seemed powerless, lay like a weight on his mind. Duncan's behaviour worried him; it seemed likely that the boy might really
be unwell. Perhaps he ought to send him to a doctor. . . . Gerald, however, had little faith in doctors. If it was "nerves" — and
there didn't seem much wrong with him physically — a doctor
would merely recommend a healthy, open-air life: and Duncan
was leading a perfectly healthy life already.

Discipline was the thing, Gerald decided, clinging to the
remnants of his own professional training: discipline, a strict

régime, were what the kid needed. But it wasn't so easy, as he had learnt from experience, to enforce anything of the kind at home. The system was too apt to break down — it was impossible for the two of them to live together on such terms. No, the boy would have to go away; but where? There were crammers, of course; and there were schools for "difficult" boys. . . . Suddenly the whole business took on, for Gerald, an air of complete futility. Duncan's dishonesty, his expulsion, seemed all at once quite unimportant. With a rare moment of vision, Gerald saw his whole life as a series of mistakes: earlier episodes recurred to him, culminating in the biggest mistake of all — the decision to be a farmer. He was no good as a farmer; he knew it at last. And since Duncan had arrived, things had gone from bad to worse. Coincidence, no doubt; but the failure of the farm and Duncan's disgrace were in some way closely connected in his mind; they appeared to him merely different aspects of the curse which had fallen upon himself and that was his; disparate symptoms, as it were, of the same disease.

A rebellious impulse seized him to make an end of the whole business: push off to Canada or Australia or somewhere, and take Duncan with him. . . . But he knew that he would do nothing of the kind. Apart from the imminent threat of war, he was in any case too lazy, nowadays, to make decisive plans for the future. At the same time, he thought, something would have to be done about Duncan. . . .

It was nearly midnight before he went up to the bedroom.

The light was still on; but Duncan lay with his eyes fast-closed on the farther side of the bed. His face was mask-like, lifeless: for a moment, Gerald was visited by the extraordinary fancy that his nephew was dead. A surge of emotion made his face flush and his body tremble: an emotion which subsided so rapidly that he couldn't identify it. Terror or exultation, pleasure or pain — it might have been either; it resembled most nearly the feeling which overcame him when the wireless-news hinted at a coming war. . . . The feeling passed, leaving him slightly sick, and shivering as though from a sudden chill.

Ridiculous, he told himself; I'm getting as morbid as the boy himself. . . . Nevertheless, he walked quietly over to the bed and examined the sleeping face more closely. He even, with an obscure sense of shame, laid his hand on Duncan's chest, over his heart. He could feel the faint pulsing, and half-laughed at himself for the sense of relief which flooded through him.

Duncan lay motionless as ever; his pyjama-jacket had slipped across his chest: he looked extraordinarily vulnerable, evoking in Gerald a sudden, peculiar sense of power. Seldom or never in his life before had he felt that any human creature was so entirely at his mercy. . . . In some remote hinterland of his mind, he was aware of danger threatening: it was like the first suspicion of some hereditary taint, creeping insidiously upon the healthy, normal consciousness.

He turned away, and began to undress. This he did, for some reason, with an unusual deliberation: laying his clothes tidily upon a chair, removing his studs and cuff-links carefully and placing them on the dressing-table. His movements were scrupulously silent, lest he should wake Duncan. At length, stripped to his shirt, he sat down gently on the other side of the bed, and reached for his pyjamas, which lay on the pillow. In the same instant, Duncan woke with a start, and made a violent movement of recoil: so violent that he nearly fell out of the bed.

"It's all right," Gerald reassured him. "It's only me."

Duncan stared back at him, his eyes glazed with terror.

"What's up?" Gerald asked, shocked at the boy's expression.

"Where am I — why are you — what——?" Duncan babbled.

"It's all right. Your bed was wet, you know. You had to get into mine. Don't you remember?"

Duncan continued to stare at him with the same blank, unrecognizing stare. Gerald reached for his hand, and gave it an affectionate squeeze.

"What's worrying you now?" he asked; his own repressed anxiety suddenly overwhelming him with a spasm of sick fear. "What's up?" he repeated.

"I don't know." Again the vague, inadequate words escaped him. "Nothing," he added.

"There's nothing else you're worried about, is there?" Gerald asked suddenly. "Nothing apart from — well, you know, this school-business, I mean."

Duncan paused for some moments, as if considering. Gerald remained where he was, squatted tentatively on the side of the bed, regarding Duncan anxiously.

"There's nothing else, I mean, that—that you're afraid to tell me?"

"I don't . . ." Duncan hesitated. "No," he said, finally. "There's nothing else. Only"—the words had a curious ring—"everything seems to have *gone* . . ."

"Gone wrong, you mean? Oh, we all feel like that sometimes. Things'll look up, you know." He pulled on his pyjama-trousers and stood up.

"No, not gone *wrong* exactly," Duncan corrected, striving to make clear to Gerald what was far from clear to himself. "Something seems to have *gone* . . ."

Gerald pulled off his shirt, and slipped on the frogged silk pyjama-jacket.

"How do you mean, gone? Was it something that happened to-night? Something that frightened you?"

"No, I don't think so. I think it was before."

"About when?"

"*I don't know.*"

"Well, never mind," Gerald said, reassuringly, climbing finally into bed, and snapping the light off. Obviously, the boy was half-dreaming, and probably a bit hysterical into the bargain. "You'll have forgotten it all in the morning," he added. Under the bedclothes he felt for Duncan's hand and squeezed it again. "Warm enough? Turn over, then, and get to sleep."

DUNCAN had been dreaming, when Gerald came to bed, that he was back in the hellebore-wood: the wood was full of small animals like weasels — they swarmed over the ground and on the branches of the beech-trees. Duncan kept remembering something he had read in a natural-history book, about how a swarm of weasels will attack a man and seize on his throat, not loosing their hold till he dies or collapses. . . . Gerald was somewhere in the dream, too: Duncan could remember, when he awoke, hearing his voice; he could even, in the moment of waking, remember the words: something about "The cliffs of fall are breaking now." In the dream they had had an immense and frightening significance, but on waking they seemed to mean nothing, after all.

He had awoken with a start of terror, the weasels at his throat: and had found himself in the big, strange bed, and Gerald sitting there in his shirt, his enormous white thighs hanging over the bed's side.

He lay now in the darkness, disquieted by the proximity of his uncle's body. The experience of the evening had set up strange echoes in his mind; the real wood was mixed up now with the dream-wood, and curious images drifted across his mind which he couldn't quite place: were they 'real,' or part of the dream? A dead rook, black and verminous; a man with the face of a fox; rain falling, falling, steadily through the darkness upon a cold, stiff body, somewhere far from home in a great boundless field.

THE boy moaned in his sleep, and turned over, pressing himself unconsciously against Gerald's body. Gerald shifted to the edge of the bed, turned over, and tried to sleep. But sleep would not come. At last, after an hour or so, he climbed gently out of bed, put on his slippers and dressing-gown, and stole guiltily downstairs.

In the dining-room he poured out a large whisky, and sat down by the ashes of the fire. Outside, the rain fell steadily. For a long time he sat motionless, staring into the cooling grate. Finally he slept, slumped down in his chair. Presently he, too, dreamed. The dream was a strange, confused travesty of the events of the evening: once again, he was pursuing his nephew through rain and darkness; but he was aware now that the wood was mined, and that enemy troops lurked in the thickets. The pursuit seemed to go on interminably, fraught with an increasing sense of guilt and terror; and all the time, he knew that it was useless, for Duncan was already dead, and the life-interest in his mother's property had reverted to himself. . . . He woke at half-past five, icy-cold, and possessed by a creeping disgust, a sense of degradation which was like a physical nausea.

After a cold bath he felt better; coming downstairs he was just in time to switch on the wireless for the early news-bulletin. The Germans were in Prague; a crisis was blowing up, apparently, over Danzig. The rich, fruity voice of the announcer sounded curiously embarrassing in the desolate morning light, like a prayer recited in some house of ill-fame.

four

THAT morning Duncan stayed in bed to breakfast. The March gale continued with unabated fierceness; the builders were telephoned for, but it was plainly impossible to start work on the roof till the weather improved. Duncan's own bed, provided with a dry mattress, was moved into his uncle's bedroom.

At lunch-time Duncan got up; he seemed little the worse for his adventure, but there was, Gerald fancied, a rather distant, preoccupied air about him.

For a day or two this look persisted, and thereafter, at irregular intervals, Gerald would notice it again: it was as though the boy were obsessed with some rather discreditable secret; at times Gerald had the impression that he was listening for something: some sound beyond the reach of normal hearing, like a bat's cry.

Duncan was, in fact, a little "off-colour" as the result of his wetting and the nervous excitement which had accompanied it. He didn't complain, however, and Gerald did not persist in his inquiries. None the less, Gerald was worried about him: perhaps he really ought to see a doctor. . . . Yet there couldn't be much wrong with him: his appetite was good, he slept well.

Analysis, whether of his own mental processes or of other people's, was not Gerald's strong point; he preferred to wait until something definite happened: then he would know how to deal with it.

At the end of a week, Duncan seemed to have more or less recovered; the weather improved, and he went riding with Sims. He was aware, however, more acutely than before, of the feeling which had haunted him for weeks past: the sense of *waiting* for some unknown and probably unpleasant event. It was probable that this accounted for his air of "listening" which his uncle had noticed; and he did, in fact, suffer more than before from the head-noises which had afflicted him since he first came to Priorsholt: noises of singing, or drumming, or the remote high humming like the wind blowing through telegraph-wires.

The sense of "waiting" was for some reason intensified by the fact that he was still sleeping in his uncle's room. The near, bodily intimacy with Gerald oppressed him with a curious, electric unrest; at night he felt compelled to lie awake until his uncle came to bed, and, pretending to be asleep, would watch him through half-closed lids as he undressed. Only when his uncle had finally got into bed and switched off the light, did he feel that it was safe to go to sleep himself.

Every other day or so, he rode with Sims or the groom. On other days he wandered, as before, through the neighbouring woods, hunting for plants. He even tried to rediscover the beech-hanger where he had found the hellebore, but all his efforts were in vain: the place seemed curiously elusive. The original bunch of hellebore drooped in a vase on his window-ledge, like a reproach; his memory of that night had become indistinct as a remembered dream, but he felt ashamed of what seemed, in retrospect, to have been an unmanly fear.

Towards the end of April, the weather grew warmer. The earliest bluebells tinged the woodland-floor, the first trickle of the azure flood to come. Purple orchises towered stiffly above them, imperial Romans among the drooping, Sabine hyacinths. The cuckoo repeated his insistent, hypnotic call in the warm afternoons. Duncan roamed the woodlands in a drowsy, unthinking mood; the feeling of suspense remained with him, accentuated by the echoing murmur in his ears, but he had become, as it were, acclimatized to the condition, and it had almost ceased to worry him.

One afternoon he walked up to the field called California: it was the first time he had visited it since the night he lost himself. Reaching the hurdle, he perceived with a start of surprise that the stones were surrounded by human figures dressed in white. A moment later, he realized that they were only soldiers, in shorts and white singlets, out for a cross-country run; they had paused (no doubt illicitly) for a brief rest, and soon ran on again, down towards the flooded valley.

Near the hurdle, a fresh batch of vermin was displayed; and nearby, on the ground, was a dead pullet, wounded in the throat. This Duncan mentioned to his uncle in the evening:

there had been several fowls missing lately. "Those damned foxes again," was Gerald's explanation.

Sometimes Duncan would come home with specimens of plants, which he placed in jam-pots on the window-ledge in his bedroom. Though Gerald did not openly show any disapproval, Duncan had a slight sense of guilt about botanizing, fancying that his uncle considered the hobby rather unmanly. In this he was, as a matter of fact, not far from the truth: though Gerald hardly analysed his own feelings in the matter, and in any case had no reasoned prejudice against botany.

The roof was repaired, and Duncan moved back to his own bedroom; but the effect of Gerald's nightly presence had produced in him an unreasonable feeling that his uncle was constantly watching him. Trivial happenings contributed to what, no doubt, was a delusion: one night he woke up suddenly to find Gerald in his room (he had come in, as it happened, to secure a rattling window); once or twice, too, his uncle had followed him rather unnecessarily, it seemed, into the bathroom; on another occasion, coming back from one of his rambles, he emerged from the woods on to the path by the house to find Gerald standing there, as though he had been waiting for him. Duncan was carrying a handful of flowers — bugle, yellow deadnettle, wood-sanicle — and, surprised in what had come to seem a slightly shameful activity, he made a motion as though to hide the flowers behind his back. Gerald said nothing, but he had noticed the gesture, and was half-aware, with an unpleasant mental after-taste, of the complex deceitfulness which it implied.

The effect of this mild persecution-mania was to provoke Duncan, perversely, into several small acts of defiance: he omitted to strip his bed in the morning before breakfast — a rule about which his uncle was particular; or he used the chamber-pot in his bedroom, another thing which Gerald had forbidden, considering it unhealthy.

He began, too, to resume on a small scale the practices which had led to his expulsion from school: he appropriated several articles belonging to Gerald and concealed them under a loose board in his bedroom-floor. A leather belt, a pair of cuff-links, an old, disused razor-strop — they were trivial thefts, and Gerald, though he did just notice the loss of one or two of the objects, and half-suspected Duncan, forebore to accuse him, partly from sheer laziness, partly because it seemed improbable that Duncan would take anything so useless. The disappearances, however, continued; and Gerald became more watchful, thereby giving some countenance to Duncan's belief that he was being spied upon.

Then, one evening, Gerald lost a packet of cigarettes.

"I left them in my room at lunch-time, I'm certain," he said to Duncan, who was reading over the fire in the sitting-room. "I remember filling my case. I suppose *you* haven't seen them?" he added, rather sharply.

"No, I haven't," Duncan replied.

Later, Gerald went upstairs to have a bath. Returning to the bedroom, a sudden thought struck him: he went into Duncan's room, and made a thorough search of it. The shelves, the bedside table, the bed itself revealed nothing; he was about to give up the search, when a loose board creaked under his foot. He leaned down and prised it up. There lay the collection of articles he had missed; and on top of them, the lost packet of cigarettes.

A flame of anger leapt in him, accompanied by a sense of triumph, almost of jubilation. He realized that this was what he had been waiting for; it was as though some pattern were about to be completed, the last piece dropped into position.

He pulled out the cigarettes, the belt, the razor-strop from their hiding-place. As he stood up, he saw Duncan himself standing in the doorway, his face a mask of terror.

Gerald felt his anger blaze to furnace-heat.

"So you *have* been at your damned tricks again!" he shouted. "I've thought so for some time. What the hell do you mean by lying to me?"

Duncan moved back a pace, staring fascinated at his uncle's face, scarlet and distorted by triumphant anger. Fresh from his bath, Gerald was naked except for a towel round his middle; Duncan noticed, with the visual alertness born of extreme fear, that the two nipples stood out stiffly, like the half-protruded horns of a snail, from the sparse black hair which surrounded them.

"I suppose you'll hardly deny that you took these, now?" Gerald thundered, holding out the packet of cigarettes. "And these too——" he held up the belt and the other articles. "I don't know what the hell made you take them; but it's just sheer downright stealing, in any case."

"I didn't mean——" Duncan began, falteringly.

"Now listen," Gerald blazed, his whole body quivering. "I want no excuses. Just tell me why you took these things?"

Duncan considered, eyeing blankly the big naked body, the distorted face.

"I don't know," he said at last.

"Oh Christ, man, can't you say any more than that? It's always the same: 'I don't know.' Well, my lad, if *you* don't know, I do: it's just plain, downright dishonesty, theft for the sake of theft."

Duncan had retreated into the outer room, and Gerald followed him, still holding the stolen articles. He placed them on the dressing-table, and noticed that his hand trembled as he did so. Anger poured over him afresh: a passion of righteous indignation. He felt a profound relief following in the wake of his fury. This, at any rate, was something he could deal with. Hysteria, "nerves" and all that were another matter: he didn't feel on safe ground. But this was just plain, wilful misbehaviour, without the least excuse.

He turned upon Duncan again.

"You know what I told you when you came home?" he said.

"I said quite plainly that if you did anything like this again, you'd be for it. Right—I meant what I said, though you may not have believed it. You've failed to keep your promise, but I intend to keep mine."

Duncan went a shade whiter.

"Do you mean—you're—you're going to——"

Gerald made an inarticulate sound.

"I'm going to give you a damned good thrashing," he exploded. "Don't you think you've bloody well deserved it?"

Duncan stood transfixed, silent, in the doorway between the two rooms.

"You'd better get undressed and go to bed," Gerald said, in a calmer tone. "I'll be up later to deal with you."

Duncan remained motionless.

"Can't you hear what I say?" Gerald snapped.

"But I didn't mean——" Duncan began.

Gerald started forward, seized the boy by his shoulders, and propelled him violently through the door.

"I want no more excuses," he said, and added, as Duncan still made no movement: "Go on—do what I tell you. Get undressed and get to bed."

There was a look of pure brutality on Gerald's face which his nephew had never seen there before. Duncan sank weakly on to the bed: fear pulsed through him with a curious rhythmic insistence—a fear not so much of being beaten, as of some other, indefinable horror exhaled by Gerald's naked body towering above him: brutal and dehumanized as some Roman gladiator poised above his fallen adversary.

"I — I'm sorry I took the — the things," Duncan muttered, half-audibly.

"It'll do you no good to start cringing," Gerald snapped. "Do as I tell you — get to bed."

He raised his arm, and Duncan ducked his head, thinking his uncle was about to strike him. Clumsily he began to pull off his clothes. The pulse of fear within him pounded like an engine, with an accelerated violence.

"Hurry up," Gerald rapped out, impatiently.

Duncan pulled off his shirt, and felt his terror spill over into an excruciating spasm that seemed beyond pleasure or pain: it was like the sensation, in a dream, of falling over a cliff. Once before he had known that same frightening sense of losing his hold — on the evening of the storm, when he had lost himself in the woods. He was lost again now: lost in a deeper and darker wood, farther from familiar country than he had ever been before.

At last Gerald turned away, and strode back into his own room, closing the door behind him. He felt suddenly extremely tired, and rather cold: the evening was chilly, and the room unheated.

He dressed quickly and went downstairs.

In the sitting-room, he helped himself to a large whisky. Then, going out to one of the outhouses, he chose a length of cane from a pile used for training raspberries. Back in the house, he took another drink. Immensely fatigued, and feeling somehow deflated, he felt his determination oozing from him. With an effort, he pulled himself together and walked upstairs.

He passed through his own bedroom, flung open the door of Duncan's, and strode across to the bed. The daylight was fading, and in the dimness Duncan's face appeared vaguely, twisted into an abnormal position upon the pillow. Looking more closely, Gerald was astounded to see that his hands were locked in the old pair of handcuffs.

"What the devil made you put *them* on?" Gerald demanded. He dropped the cane, and bent forward to release the trapped hands. As he seized them, Duncan began to struggle wildly, without a sound: precisely as Gerald had often seen some small animal struggling in a trap. With difficulty, Gerald managed to unlock the handcuffs, and the boy recoiled violently against the wall.

"Leave me alone," he cried, in a high, sharpened voice. "Let me go —" as Gerald seized him afresh, in an effort to restrain his wild movements.

"It's all right," Gerald said, quietly. "I'm not going to hurt you. Whatever possessed you to fasten yourself up like that?"

Once again Duncan struggled to free himself, but Gerald clasped him firmly, passing his hand round the narrow shoulders, and pinioning his arms.

"It's all right," Gerald repeated gently. "Why are you so

frightened? You must learn to take your punishment, you know — you mustn't funk these things. Being a funk's nearly as bad as being dishonest."

Gerald broke off, feeling the inadequacy of his words. The boy was obviously no more aware of what was being said to him than a wounded animal. Gerald loosened his grip, and at the same time felt the taut body relax. Almost simultaneously Duncan began to sob.

Relieved, Gerald held him gently in his arms. The outburst of violence had frightened him: for a moment he had thought that Duncan had really had some kind of seizure.

"Why are you so frightened?" he asked again.

Duncan's eyes looked up at his, vague and blurred in the dim light.

"I thought — when you came in — I thought — " for a moment his sobs prevented him from finishing the sentence. Then, in a curiously flat voice, he said: "I thought you were going to kill me."

Gerald started, relaxing his hold on the boy's body.

"What? What's that?"

The incredible words were repeated, in an identical tone: cold, expressionless. Gerald was immensely shocked: suddenly brought face to face with abnormality, his whole "official" attitude collapsed, he felt frightened and ineffectual, as though he were a child himself. He pulled himself together: the boy was hysterical, obviously.

"What nonsense," Gerald exclaimed. "You don't know what you're saying."

Duncan looked at him, flicking his eyelids which were still wet with tears; but he had stopped crying now.

"I thought you wanted to," he said.

"Look here, you're being ridiculous." Gerald pressed him closer. "I intended to beat you because you disobeyed. You've behaved dishonestly, and incidentally broken your promise to me. You also told me a lie. You've been beaten at school: you know perfectly well that nobody wants to do it. Nobody *wants* to make you unhappy at all; but you've got to be taught a lesson."

Duncan considered this. Then, in the same inexpressive tone, he spoke again.

"Nobody's ever hated me before, like you do."

Gerald had a disquieting sensation as of some seismic disturbance in his mind: his whole scale of values seemed suddenly displaced, and for a moment he felt himself trembling on the verge of an abyss. He gaped at Duncan incredulously.

"You little idiot — you know perfectly well how fond I am of you. . . . At least, I thought you knew. I even thought you — you quite liked me. Hate you indeed! Why, I — I'm fonder of you than anybody in the world, if you must know."

Duncan looked drowsy, and rather bored with the discussion.

"It's the same thing," he muttered, sleepily.

Gerald thought that he must have misheard his words. The remark seemed meaningless.

"What's that you say?" he asked.

"Nothing."

Duncan had almost forgotten, himself, what he had said. The sense of his words remained with him, however: a curious feeling that nothing mattered, everything was the same, finally — hating, loving, all the rest of it. The separate words had lost their meaning, merged into an engulfing nothingness. He felt extremely tired, and wished Gerald would get the business over and leave him alone.

Gerald laid him gently back on the pillow, and rose to his feet. He picked up the cane, which he had dropped on the floor when he came in, and, flexing his knee, broke it sharply into two pieces.

"You'd better turn over now and try to get to sleep," he said. "I'll send Sims up with something to eat later."

"Aren't you going to ——" Duncan began, and broke off, questioningly.

Gerald turned to him.

"You seem to have punished yourself enough for the moment," he said. "I don't know if you're just funking, or what's up with you. In any case, we'll talk about it tomorrow."

Gerald turned away, and went downstairs. The whole business had shocked him deeply; the sense of "displacement," of shifting frontiers, lingered in his mind, setting up ominous

echoes. "Hysteria," "nerves," "abnormality" — the words rat-
tled emptily through his brain, meaningless counters explaining nothing. Up till now, he had ignored Duncan's peculiari-
ties, preferring to "wait till something happened." Now
something had indeed happened, but he was as much in the
dark as ever: more so, in fact. What was it the boy had said? "It's
all the same" — no, "It's the same thing." Meaningless nonsense. And the idea that one wanted to kill him. . . . And what
on earth had possessed him to fasten himself up with those
handcuffs? It was certainly time, Gerald decided, that he saw a
doctor.

Wearily, with a feeling of complete futility, Gerald went to
the dining-room, and poured out a drink. Formerly a strictly
moderate, if regular, drinker, he realized that he was fast becoming an habitual toper. But somehow it didn't seem particularly important.

Outside, the April evening was loud with the singing of birds.
On the untended lawn below the window, the lent-lilies hung
like small, partially unfurled flags: half-hearted celebrants of
the chilly English spring. Gerald poured out another whisky —
neat this time — and gulped it down like a bitter draught. Then
he sat down by the fireplace, staring sightlessly out of the window into the fading brightness.

five

WITH a queer sense of hopelessness, Gerald allowed the matter of Duncan's punishment to drop—or almost drop. On the day following, an interview did take place between uncle and nephew; but it was a singularly meaningless ceremony, and rather embarrassing to both parties. Duncan was to do an hour's extra work a day for the next week; Gerald also exacted from him a fresh promise to do nothing dishonest.

A peculiarly artificial relationship sprang up between the two of them. By tacit agreement, they avoided each other as much as possible. Duncan was polite and well-behaved; Gerald tried his best to be his normal self. He would greet Duncan with perfect good-humour whenever he encountered him, but would soon fall silent, and, on one pretext or another, hurry out of his presence. Seeing the boy behaving with apparent normality, he began to hope that things had really taken a turn for the better; but at the back of his mind he was sceptical: Duncan's extraordinary behaviour had convinced him that the boy was in some way profoundly abnormal.

As for Duncan, the episode remained in his mind like the

memory of a recent illness, from which his constitution seemed to have recovered, but which had left him, as it were, minus some vital organ or secretion: a part of his mind had simply ceased to function. Just as an amputation-case will attempt, long after the operation, to make use of the missing limb, so Duncan found himself, in face of certain mental experiences, suddenly brought up short, aware of a total loss of capacity. The actual events of that evening had quickly been forgotten: or rather, not forgotten, but insulated in some remote part of his mind, just as some physical focus of infection may become fibrosed or encysted, and thus, for the time being, harmless to the rest of the system.

APRIL turned to May, and the first hot days came. Gerald's growing preoccupation with the farm-work left him little time to devote to his nephew; and Duncan found that he was free to do very much as he chose. He even formed the habit of saddling the pony and riding out by himself; perhaps Gerald was un-aware of this, but in any case he made no objection.

In the mornings, too, when he was supposed to be working, Duncan took to slipping out unseen and hiding himself in the woods. On one or two occasions Gerald must have observed these truant escapes; but he made no comment. Where Duncan was concerned, he had become, latterly, curiously defeatist.

In the warm evenings, after dinner, Gerald would pull his

chair to the open window, the whisky and syphon on a table by his side. Usually Duncan contrived to slip away after the meal, for he found his uncle's company faintly embarrassing, nowadays — a feeling which, indeed, Gerald appeared to reciprocate.

One evening, however, just as Duncan was leaving the room, Gerald called him back.

"Where are you running off to?" he asked. "You don't seem able to sit still a minute nowadays. Can't you take it easy for a change — read a book or something?"

Without replying, Duncan took up an old volume of the *Illustrated London News* and sat down with it in the window-seat. Gerald's mild outburst was occasioned merely by a passing fit of irritability; no sooner had he spoken, than he regretted having done so. Duncan's presence, self-consciously obedient yet subtly mutinous, embarrassed him.

From his seat he watched the boy narrowly; and after a few minutes saw him raise his head, cocking his ear as though listening to some distant sound.

Irritated, and faintly disturbed, Gerald extended his leg and touched the boy's body with his foot to draw his attention.

"What's up? Hear something?" he asked.

Duncan nodded.

"It sounded like — like a horn or something."

"Car, probably."

"No, it was playing — sort of music."

"Oh, a bugle, then. There *are* some troops in camp, somewhere up beyond the wood. I don't know where exactly."

"But it's not *only* that — sometimes there's a kind of singing noise." Duncan spoke nervously, turning his face away.

"Well, soldiers do sing, you know, quite often."

"Yes, but there *weren't* any soldiers — not then, when I first heard it."

"When was that?"

"When I first came here — last — I mean, Christmas time."

Gerald stiffened in his chair. He was faced, once more, by the abnormal: and flinched at the encounter. In the dim light his eyes met Duncan's, and a singular look passed between them. It was as if their souls, momentarily disembodied, had suddenly come face to face, meeting each other nakedly, shamefully, in a setting of some shared, secret degradation. It was only for a brief moment: almost instantly, normality reasserted itself, and Gerald laughed.

"You must have been imagining things," he said.

"Perhaps I was," Duncan agreed, in the tone of one who wishes to believe in something against the evidence of reason.

Gerald poured him out half a glass of port.

"Drink that, my son, and don't get imagining things," Gerald said.

No further reference was made that night to Duncan's "noises." But the next morning Gerald made an appointment with a doctor in Glamber.

AS Gerald had hoped and expected, the doctor's verdict was entirely satisfactory. Gerald had had a talk to him before he saw Duncan: he had told him of the boy's "nerviness," and also given a somewhat soft-pedalled version of his expulsion from school; he omitted, however, to mention Duncan's more recent lapses, and their peculiar sequel.

There was nothing organically wrong, the doctor told Gerald, after the examination. The boy was highly strung, a bit "nervy" — there was a history of meningitis which went far to explain this — and probably he was growing too fast. Plenty of fresh air and exercise, and good food — one couldn't do more than that at present. A tonic was prescribed. The doctor added, in answer to Gerald's query, that there was no harm at all in half a glass of port after dinner. . . .

Gerald's relief was immense. He had done the right thing — and he had been rewarded; his conscience was now clear. If a certain uneasiness lingered, it was easily dealt with: as easily as the sense of guilt in one who has just confessed and been absolved.

Relieved, in part, of the problem of his nephew, Gerald was still faced by the slow but certain failure of the farm. He sold some shares for the sake of a few immediate improvements, but his action would probably, he thought, turn out a dead loss. He asked advice from neighbours in a new spirit of humility; but his attitude in the past had been too arrogant, too "county" altogether, for his humble-pie to command much sympathy.

ONE evening, escaping from the house after dinner, Duncan took the path up towards the woods. It was moonlight, and the way showed clearly; the May night was warm, caressing pleasantly his bare arms and throat. Once in the wood, he stopped, straining his ears; from somewhere far off, over the hill, came a noise of singing. Accustomed to the intermittent head-noises which haunted him, he stood stock-still for several minutes, doubting the reality of what he heard. But on this occasion, at least, the sounds were perfectly genuine.

Half-frightened, almost inclined to turn back, he walked slowly on up the woodland path. As he neared the hurdle leading into the field, he detected a light—several lights—shining faintly through the trees. Soon he reached the path's end, and stood there transfixed: overcome by a feeling of intense, rather horrible excitement. His knees trembled, he clung to the hurdle for support. His emotion was tinged with a queer sense of inevitability: it was as though some ancient prophecy had at last been fulfilled.

Round the margin of the field, lights glowed beneath the trees, and human figures, dimly discernible, moved between the lights. Somewhere voices were raised in a song. Duncan leaned over the hurdle, straining eyes and ears towards the lights and movement, possessed by a profound thankfulness, a sense of some intolerable strain suddenly relaxed.

His long period of waiting was rewarded: the field was tenanted at last, the stones were no longer alone.

WHEN Duncan returned, much later, to the house, Gerald was waiting for him. He was struck by the expression on the boy's face: a look of restrained, triumphant excitement.

"What's up? Where have you been all this time?" he asked. Duncan looked evasive.

"Come on, tell me. It's not a secret, is it?" Gerald insisted.

"I went up to the field with the stones," Duncan murmured, reluctantly.

"Oh, there's some troops in camp there, aren't there? I was up that way today — I saw the tents."

Duncan turned away, with a look of peculiar slyness, and walked upstairs to his bedroom.

THE next day Gerald was to drive, on business, to the other end of the county, and would not be back till late. Duncan had his supper alone, and afterwards, filled with a strange excitement, walked up the path through the woods.

It was a dull evening, threatening rain: a high ceiling of grey cloud covered the sky, and chilly breezes wavered fitfully through the hazel-thickets. In the grey, subdued light, the young green glowed with a curious, self-generated brilliance; beneath the trees, each vista was dimmed by the watery, greyish haze of the bluebells. A cuckoo called insistently, long after the other birds were silent.

When Duncan reached the entrance to the field, it seemed

at first that its occupants had departed: soon, however, he perceived the camouflaged bell-tents beneath the trees, and khaki
figures moving among them. A bugle struck up, sounding the
tattoo: high and clear, piercing the woodland stillness with an
erotic nostalgia.

Duncan crept round the fringe of the wood till he reached
the three ivy-covered barrows. Here he was within hearing-
distance of the nearest tents, and could just see, in the dim light,
two of the soldiers sitting on upturned boxes, polishing the
buttons on their tunics. Their voices came to him indistinctly:
he could hear little of what they were saying, but, slightly
shocked, was able to detect the monotonous recurrence of a
single obscene word. It reminded him of the private "lan-
guages" which they used to coin at his prep. school, in which
each word or letter was followed by some meaningless mono-
syllable, producing, upon the uninitiated, an effect of complete
gibberish.

Presently one of the soldiers left the other, and carried his
tunic into the tent. In a few minutes he reappeared, and, after
exchanging a complicit wink with his friend, began to move
rather furtively, with several backward glances, towards the
wood. He climbed the fence, and walked softly forward between the mounds. He started slightly on seeing Duncan, but
quickly recovering his self-possession, nodded good evening.

Duncan stared up at him, struck speechless by a violent, incredulous excitement; for he had recognized, in the dimly seen figure, the soldier whom he had met in the train, months ago, on his first journey to Priorsholt.

"Lookin' for someone, mate?" asked the soldier, who had not recognized him.

Duncan came closer.

"Don't you remember me?" he asked.

The man stared back, startled, at the white face, crowned with red hair, mutely pleading in the vague, bluish dusk.

"I can't say as I do —"

"I met you in the train," Duncan explained rapidly. "Last hols — I mean, just before Christmas. You said you were going to Glamber and you gave me a cigarette. Your name's Jim Tylor."

"Well, I'll be —!" the soldier exclaimed. " 'Course I remember — you was in trouble, like — lost your Ma. I can't just recall your moniker —"

"Duncan."

"That's right! You was comin' to these parts to live with your auntie, ain't that right?"

"My uncle," Duncan corrected.

"Well, if that ain't queer. Fancy you turnin' up 'ere like this. Proper coincidence, ain't it?"

Duncan found speech suddenly difficult; the soldier, too, was silent. The dusk was thickening: lights appeared in the camp. Hesitant, motionless in the dim light, the man and the boy stood there looking at each other, uneasily. Duncan noticed that the soldier's bare arms were elaborately tattooed; his chest, too, half-visible beneath the gaping shirt, was patterned with some obscure design.

"Well, it's nice to have met you again," the man said awkwardly.

"It's nice to meet you," Duncan echoed.

"Just havin' a walk out, eh?" the other queried, uneasy. "Not much of a night for walkin' — feels like rain to me."

"Where were *you* going?" Duncan asked, rather anxiously.

The soldier looked evasive.

"Just got a bit of a job to see after," he muttered. "Look 'ere, kid," he added, persuasively, "it's time you was getting home. The folks 'll be wonderin' where you've got to, else."

"I'm going down through the wood," Duncan explained. With unaccustomed boldness he added, "Can't I come with you?"

He hung on the answer as though enormous issues depended from it. Suddenly it had become immensely important to him that the brief friendship struck up in the train should be renewed.

The man stared back at him, dubious, plainly wishing him out of the way. But Duncan stood his ground.

"Can't I?" he repeated.

Again, the other hesitated.

"See here," he said at last. "Can you keep a secret?"

"Yes, of course I can," said Duncan quickly.

"Well, look 'ere then: you can come along with me, but you don't see nothing of what I'm doing, see? See nothing and hear nothing — understand?"

Curiously thrilled, Duncan assented briefly.

"Fact is" — the man lowered his voice — "I'm after the bunnies. Used to be a fair hand at that, back in Civvy Street. Comes in useful, times like this. But they'll have me over the wall if I'm copped."

"O.K., I won't say anything," Duncan repeated.

"Promise — word of honour?"

"On my word of honour."

"That's all right, then, kid. Where do you live around here?"

"I live down at the bottom of the wood — Priorsholt's the name of the house."

"What, you live at the farm, do you?" The soldier whistled. "Well, listen, son: not a word to nobody, see?"

"I've given you my word of honour," Duncan reminded him.

"O.K., kid. I can see you're all right. Only we got to be careful, see?" Secretly, he was wondering if the boy could be of any use, and decided that he might be. "I daresay you know the lie of the land pretty fair, then, eh?" he questioned.

"Pretty well," Duncan admitted.

"All right: come on then."

The soldier leading, they crept silently down a narrow track which Duncan did not know. The boy's heart beat with such violence that it seemed as if it must be audible. The soldier wore rubber shoes, and Duncan, following behind, almost bit his tongue out in his efforts to walk without sound.

Presently the track was crossed by another; they must be somewhere near the beech-hanger, Duncan thought.

"One of the runs is just here," the soldier whispered. "Here we are. No, nothin' doin' this time, sod it." He adjusted the noose, artfully concealed, by the dim light of a pocket-torch, masked with dark paper: explaining the process to Duncan as he did so. "I expect you're up to all these tricks, livin' in the country," he added, flatteringly.

"We'll try the next one," he said, and they moved forward again. "Got him this time, the little ——" he exclaimed. "Only a little 'un, but better than nowt." Seizing the rabbit firmly, he picked up a heavy stone and struck its head: stuffing the body into his shirt-front, next to his skin.

"What do you do with them—eat them?" Duncan asked.

The soldier glanced at him sharply.

"Flog the pelts," he replied briefly. "Bloke up where I come from used to give us one-and-a-tanner a time. Can't expect to get that in these parts. But it's good sport, apart from the dough."

By the time they turned back, the total bag was four rabbits. Duncan walked with his new friend as far as the mounds, and here they parted.

"Now mind, not a word to nobody," the soldier repeated. He hesitated, considering possibilities. The kid might be useful, living on the farm, he reflected. "Want to come out again?" he suggested.

"I'd love to," Duncan replied. It was what he had hoped for — yet scarcely dared to hope.

"O.K., then. Tomorrow night. Same time. Same place. Cheerioh, kid. Pleased to have met you again."

He turned away, and Duncan started back, in a state of high excitement, down the homeward path.

URING the next few weeks his new-found friend possessed Duncan's heart entirely. On the evenings when Jim Tylor was on duty or had gone into the town, Duncan mooned about miserably, unable to occupy himself with anything else. On other nights he would steal out after dinner, in gym-shoes, to the appointed meeting-place, and accompany Jim on his poaching-expeditions.

With practice he became of some considerable use to his friend, and Jim, with an eye to other possible advantages, encouraged him. After the first few meetings he took Duncan into his confidence: he had a good market in the town, and not only for rabbits, either—he was out for all he could get in the poaching line.

Flattered by his confidence, Duncan did his best to be useful. His promise of secrecy was kept absolutely. Gerald, if he noticed his prolonged absences at night, seldom made any comment, beyond a grunt of disapproval. He had, in fact, noticed that Duncan was behaving oddly and secretively; also, that he was undergoing a physical change, becoming coarser in the face, and rougher and more careless in his habits. He neglected his nails, and his clothes were often filthy. But he looked healthier, and this was enough for Gerald. It would do the boy no harm to run wild for a bit longer, he thought: a convenient view, so far as himself was concerned, for the farm occupied all his energies. Once, when in London, he took the trouble to inquire about emigration-schemes, and actually wrote to an old friend who was now farming in Canada, asking for his advice.

For Duncan, Jim Tylor became a personification of romance and adventure. The secret "island" of his phantasies seemed nowadays almost to have lost its identity: the saga had become discredited by the impact of reality, had merged itself into the exciting actuality of the poaching-expeditions in the soldier's company.

No detail of Jim's life was too trivial to be of interest to his young friend. Duncan began, indeed, in phantasy, to lead the life of a soldier; by listening to Jim's talk, and watching, from the outside, his daily routine, he had familiarized himself to an extraordinary extent with the details of Army life. Merely to watch Jim cleaning his rifle, and to hear him explain its workings, was a matter of passionate interest to him: and all the minor happenings of his existence — the parades, the punishments, the eternal spit-and-polish — were invested with an atmosphere of high romance.

Jim's complaints about Army food were violent and unremitting; he seemed always hungry. It was not long before Duncan had learned to take the hint. He began in a small way:

smuggling bread-and-jam and cake out of the dining-room at
meal-times. Encouraged by Jim's gratitude, he became bolder
and, on one or two occasions, raided the larder. The knuckle-
end of a ham, some cooked sausages and a potted tongue were
delivered up to his hungry friend, whose full-hearted thanks
Duncan found a more than sufficient reward.

Sims and the daily maid were puzzled by the disappearances; it was some time, however, before the matter came to
Gerald's ears. When the reports did reach him, he dealt with the
affair briefly and violently.

"Did you pinch these things?" he snapped at Duncan one
morning.

"No." Duncan lied boldly, staring him full in the eyes.

"Well, just let me catch you, and you know what you're in
for," Gerald retorted, unconvinced. "And mind, I'm not letting
you off a second time."

Later in the day, when Duncan was out, Gerald searched his
room, but without result. There was nothing much more he
could do; habitually, nowadays, he found himself shelving the
problem of his nephew's upbringing. Something, he felt, would
sooner or later happen to put things right. Meanwhile, he had
no time to worry about such secondary matters; work kept him
fully occupied.

TO Duncan, his new friend had come to seem, among other
things, a kind of ally against his uncle. He was aware that be-

tween himself and Gerald there had existed, for some time, a state of undeclared war: a conflict which was carried on, as it were, behind the scenes, an affair of diplomacy and secret treaties which might, none the less, flare up at any time into an overt battle.

In this "warfare" he felt Jim, the soldier, to be mustered on his side; at the same time regarding him as a kind of chosen leader to whom he had sworn fealty. The thefts of food were so many secret assaults upon enemy territory — as, indeed, were also the poaching-expeditions themselves, for the wood belonged to Gerald.

One evening Jim greeted him at the edge of the camp with a sly, complicit grin.

"See here, kid, I got an idea. You like a bit of sport, same as me, don't you?"

Duncan nodded.

"And you ain't all that struck on your uncle, neither, from what you've told me — eh?"

Again Duncan nodded.

"Well, see 'ere: what's to stop us baggin' a couple of nice young pullets, for instance?"

Duncan looked puzzled.

"Do you mean from the farm?"

"That's right. It's an easy enough job, but I'd want your help, see?" Jim gave a long wink. "I know you're one of the wide boys," he added.

He was consciously playing on Duncan's romantic idea of

himself in the rôle of criminal. Even as he spoke, he saw the boy's eyes light up with a flame of excitement.

"All right," Duncan agreed — envisaging, as it were, a new and more audacious assault upon the enemy's defences.

Jim already had a plan ready. Duncan was to let him in at the side-gate, about midnight; he could slip in without anyone being the wiser. The birds would have to be killed at once, on the premises. Duncan would act as guide to the hen-roost; Jim would bring a sharp knife with him.

"It's best to slit its throat," he explained. "Makes too much noise, t'other way."

The question remained which night would be most suitable. Duncan remembered that tomorrow was Saturday and that his uncle would be going to London for the week-end. There shouldn't be too much danger with Gerald out of the house; Sims slept on the top floor, and none of the farm-hands lived within hearing.

"Okeydoke, then — we'll make it tomorrow," Jim said, finally.

DUNCAN slept little that night; for hours he lay rehearsing over and over again what he had to do. It was easy enough, but the sense of danger made his heart beat with a painful violence. Raids on the larder had been a different matter — mere routine patrols into enemy territory. This was to be a deliberate act of war.

The next day his painful, overmastering excitement continued; by the evening he felt dead-tired, but his nervous tension kept him wide-awake.

Everything, as it happened, went according to plan. At midnight, Duncan satisfied himself that Sims was in bed, and that nobody else was about. Then he stole down to the side-gate. Presently Jim emerged from the darkness.

"Everything O.K.?" he whispered.

"Yes. The shed's just over here."

Jim followed him. Duncan opened the door, and the soldier flashed his masked light on the sleeping fowls, examining them with an expert eye.

"Them two'll do," he muttered. "All ready? One at a time, then. Here goes for number one." He seized one of the birds, and stepped quickly out of the hut. Duncan was appalled at the squawking and fluttering: it seemed as though the whole farm must wake up. It was only for a moment, however; while Duncan held the torch, Jim made a swift incision: the hen continued to struggle for what seemed like an interminable time. "O.K.— she'll do," Jim said at last, and went back to the hut. The other bird was soon dispatched. Jim stuffed the carcases unceremoniously into the front of his battle-dress tunic. He looked curiously sullen and unfriendly, and seemed in a hurry to be off. By the light of the torch, Duncan saw that his hands were covered with blood. He was turning away without even saying good night, when Duncan mustered the courage to speak.

"What about tomorrow?" he asked, suddenly, desolate at his friend's lack of warmth.

"Tomorrow?" The soldier looked at him vaguely, impatient to be gone.

"Yes. Shan't I come up?"

"Oh, ay. Come up about nine — the usual place." He turned away abruptly, and disappeared into the darkness. Duncan returned to the hut, and kicked some earth over the traces of blood and feathers outside the door. The night seemed suddenly disturbed: a pheasant squawked in the wood, and an owl began to hoot. A gust of wind rose suddenly and subsided again as Duncan walked back to the house.

NEXT evening Duncan was at the appointed rendezvous, but there was no sign of Jim. He waited an hour or more, then miserably turned homeward, wondering what he had done to antagonize his friend.

Mid-June had come with hot, unsettled weather: thunder haunted the distance, muttering round the horizon like the sound of a far battle. Gerald was overwrought and bad-tempered, and snapped at his nephew with an increasing frequency. More often than not, he went out in the evening, driving over to Glamber or Cliffhaven, and buying drinks which he guiltily knew he couldn't afford. A strange restlessness consumed him. Business was no better, and the problem of Duncan remained to be dealt with: it was high time the kid went to school; yet Gerald continued to shelve the matter. Meanwhile the boy's presence irritated him and made him more restless than ever. From something Sims had said, he suspected him of making friends with some of the soldiers at the camp; doubtless he was up to no good. He had developed, Gerald thought, an air of increased slyness, and he had a remarkable capacity for disappearing whenever his uncle was at home.

The farm-hand responsible for the fowls reported the loss of two pullets.

"Those confounded foxes again, I suppose," Gerald said.

"It didn't look like foxes," the man replied.

"Well, what did it look like?"

"More as if someone had broken in. Shouldn't wonder if it was them soldiers."

Restless, weighed down by a chronic fatigue, Gerald soon forgot the incident. The soldiers, in any case, would be going soon: he had heard the news from one of their officers. That night he drove into Glamber and dined at the Grand Hotel, where he fell in with some other Army acquaintances.

"It looks as if we're bound to have a scrap before the autumn," they said.

A FEW nights later Duncan, wandering without much hope near the three barrows at the top of the wood, encountered Jim Tylor.

The soldier greeted him with almost more than his usual friendliness.

"H'llo, kid—haven't seen you lately. What's been up?"

Duncan regarded him searchingly: a profound relief flooded

through his mind; at the same time, he remembered uneasily Jim's sullen off-hand manner at their last meeting.

"I — I thought you might not want to see me," Duncan muttered uncertainly.

"Not want to see you? Why, we're pals, ain't we?" He ran his hand playfully over Duncan's hair. "I'm always glad to see you, kid."

The longest day was near; but tonight was cloudy and moonless, and under the trees it was almost dark. The woods were oppressive, hot and fly-haunted; sudden gusts of wind struck the thickets at intervals, subsiding abruptly, and leaving the air more stagnant than before.

"Come on, then," Jim suggested. "What say we goes and has a look at the runs?"

They started down the path: the deeper darkness folded itself about them, and the heat was almost unbearable. Following closely on the soldier's heels, Duncan could detect, more clearly than usual, the sour, animal smell of his body. They explored the usual runs; but without success.

"No bloody luck," Jim commented, when they had drawn blank half a dozen times. "It's them — keepers." They had reached a small clearing, and the soldier planted himself on a fallen log, and lit a cigarette. He offered one to Duncan, who accepted, and sat down close beside him.

They smoked in silence. Duncan, who had taken to the habit more for the sake of imitating his friend than because of any pleasure it gave him, soon finished his cigarette and stubbed it out. He sat watching Jim's face as it appeared intermittently, in the faint red glow. The night's oppression seemed to increase; one could imagine, in the darkness, that the thickly clouded sky was pressing downwards, like a heavy quilt, upon the tree-tops. Duncan could feel the warmth from Jim's thick, solid body at his side; sitting there, in a ponderous silence, the soldier seemed to have drawn the night about him like a cloak. Habited in darkness, he seemed the night's centre, a living, sensual core of warmth and mystery.

Presently he broke the silence, with a single obscene expression of disgust.

"Oh —— it," he muttered, and stubbed out his cigarette on the tree-trunk.

"What's up?" Duncan asked, sympathetically.

"Nowt more than usual," Jim replied. "Just browned-off to the teeth." He paused. "I'm broke this week, and all," he added flatly.

"Do you mean you want some money?"

Jim laughed.

"That's about the idea. I suppose we all do, come to that. Still, I won't starve in the bloody Army, when all's said and done." He paused, a thought suddenly striking him; then continued: "Fact is, it's a bit awkward this week — I owes one of the blokes thirty bob, and he's sort of getting anxious. I suppose——" he broke off; then, as Duncan made no answer, he placed his hand on the boy's knee and squeezed it. "I suppose you don't happen to be flush at the moment?" he ventured.

Duncan paused.

"How much do you want?" he asked at length.

"Oh well——" Jim spoke with a careful casualness. "If you could manage a quid or two. . . . It's only just to tide over. Payday's on Friday—I could let you have it back then."

Duncan hesitated. A quid or two! He had imagined that Jim would be satisfied with half-a-crown or five bob. Plainly his own pocket-money wouldn't help much.

"How about it, eh?" Jim muttered, insinuatingly, his hand still clasping the boy's knee.

"All right," said Duncan suddenly, with decision. "I'll bring it to you tomorrow or the next day. Will that do?"

"Cor, you're a proper toff." Jim's hand tightened again on his knee. In the darkness the soldier grinned to himself, amused at the boy's innocence. He was a useful bit of goods, and no mistake.

PRESENTLY Duncan left him and walked thoughtfully down through the wood. He had made his promise without the faintest idea of how he was to fulfil it. Borrowing from Gerald was impossible: his uncle would ask too many questions. Perhaps Sims would lend him a pound or two. But Sims, too, might reasonably want to know what he wanted it for. It wasn't as if he would really be able to pay it back: he had no illusions — not of this kind, at least — about Jim Tylor. But he had made a promise; and he had every intention of keeping it.

That night he lay awake for a long time in the hot, airless darkness. An idea had occurred to him: an idea audacious in its simplicity. It would be highly dangerous, and would have to be carried out carefully; but it was the only way in which he could keep his promise.

Next day he waited for his opportunity; but none occurred. On the day following, Gerald was to go to London for two nights: the thing would have to be done before he went.

On the morning of his departure Gerald was astir early. Hearing him cross the landing to the bathroom, Duncan slipped out of bed and entered his uncle's room. Luck was in his way: Gerald's note-case lay on the dressing-table.

Rapidly, Duncan opened the case and examined the contents. A sizeable wad of notes reassured him; he didn't bother to count them, and relied on Gerald himself not doing so, at least until he had left the house. He slipped out two pound notes, and replaced the wallet exactly as he had found it. Ten minutes later, when Gerald banged on his door, he pretended to be soundly asleep.

GERALD hurried away to his train after an early breakfast; and Duncan watched his departure with an immense relief. So far, so good. Leaning out of his bedroom window, he drew from his pocket a cigarette which Jim had given him, and lit it. It was risky, he knew; the smell was bound to linger in the room. Carefully, he blew the smoke out of the window. He was filled with an acute, an almost sensual excitement. The cigarette was a symbol of the new emancipation which Jim had effected in him. The thought of giving his friend the money was like an intoxication. He was not aware of the slightest sense of guilt: the soldier's personality imposed its own code—any action performed in his interest became, automatically, a moral one.

He spent the morning riding. It was a day of thundery heat: the sky was overcast, but the sun emerged at intervals, blazing out with sudden ferocity and making the damp woods steam like a Turkish bath. After lunch, Duncan walked up to the camp, on the chance of finding Jim off duty. He lingered about the tumuli for some time, and was at last rewarded by seeing his friend emerge from the tent. He signalled to him discreetly.

Jim grinned across, and winked at him. In a minute or two he came over and joined Duncan, who hurriedly pulled him round behind the mounds, out of sight of the camp.

"Here you are," he said, and handed over the two notes.

"I say, you're a bloody toff," Jim exclaimed. He stowed the money away somewhat hurriedly, and flung his arm round the boy's shoulder. "Proper bloody toff, that's what you are. It's uncommon nice of you, kid."

"That's all right," Duncan murmured.

"See here, though" — Jim's face suddenly took on a rather unconvincing expression of gravity — "will it be O.K. if I send it on to you?"

Duncan looked at him, puzzled.

"Fact is, you see," Jim continued, "we're moving off sooner than what I thought, and we won't get paid out before we go."

Duncan's heart sank like a stone.

"When are you going?" he asked in a small voice.

"Tomorrow," Jim replied. "Sorry, kid — I won't forget to send it on."

"It's not the money," Duncan murmured, almost speechless with the weight of his unhappiness. "I don't want it — it's not mine."

"Not yours, eh?" Jim queried.

"No," Duncan looked up at the strong, sunburnt face with a curious pride. Jim winked at him meaningly.

"Got it off your uncle, did you?"

Duncan nodded.

Jim gave a whistle, and his face broke into a slyly appreciative grin.

"You're coming on, kid, ain't you?" he said.

Duncan blushed, feeling pleasure tingle through him like a draught of wine. It was worth any risk, he felt, to receive such praise from his friend. . . . But Jim was going away; the knowledge struck at him afresh, extinguishing his moment's happiness. A cloud passed over the sun: the afternoon seemed suddenly dark.

"What time do you go tomorrow?" he asked hopelessly.

Jim shrugged his shoulders.

"Sometime in the mornin'," he said. "We're striking camp at reveille."

"Where are you going?"

"Back to Glamber—back into barracks again. . . . Roll on my next leaf."

Duncan was silent for a moment. Then he felt the soldier touch his arm.

"Come over and have a sit-down," he said. "I'm all alone—s'posed to be tent-orderly. The other blokes is out on a ——ing route-march."

Duncan followed his friend over the fence, into the camp. There seemed very few soldiers about. Jim held the tent-flap aside for him, and he went in. The tent, with the sun beating directly on to the canvas, was hot as an oven. Jim pointed to a blanket-roll.

"Sit yourself down," he said.

Duncan obeyed, and Jim squatted on a kit-bag.

"It's ——ing hot," he said. "Have a fag." They lit cigarettes. Jim was sweating, and he unbuttoned his thick, Angola shirt to the waist. Duncan stared, oddly fascinated, at the elaborate pattern which covered the white, muscular chest: a heart pierced by a dagger, and encircled by a snake.

"Looking at the old picture-gallery, eh?" Jim said, laughing across at him. "Had that one done in Alex. These 'ere"—he held out his forearms—"I had *them* done in Marseilles. I got one on me back, too—I'll show you if you like." He stood up and stripped off his shirt, displaying, on his broad back, a carefully executed design of a naked woman. "Bit of all right, eh? Pity I can't see it."

He was obviously extremely proud of his decorations.

"Quite a bleedin' art-gallery, eh?" he laughed. "I'll show you my photos, if you like." He fumbled in his kit and at last produced a grubby packet, which he handed to his visitor.

Duncan turned them over curiously: there were views of Alexandria and Cairo; snapshots of Jim and his friends, of his mother and father; more pictures of Jim—in walking-out kit, in bathing-drawers, dressed for football. Among the photographs, Duncan came on a smaller packet, wrapped in grubby tissue-paper. As he was undoing it, Jim laid a restraining hand on his.

"I dunno as you ought to look at them ones," he said with a chuckle.

But the photographs had already slid from the paper. Duncan glanced at them, then bent forward with a sudden, concentrated eagerness. They were the standard pornographic article—bought probably in Alexandria; but to Duncan they came with all the shock of complete novelty. Things which, for the past year or so, he had sometimes vaguely imagined in his secret phantasies; things which, when he thought about them at all, he had believed wholly peculiar to his own imagination—here they were, in horrifying physical fact, fixed by the camera and vulgarized into a laughable grotesqueness.

"Pretty hot stuff, eh?" Jim laughed.

His cheeks flaming, Duncan looked up timidly at his friend. Jim grinned back at him, rubbing his hand across his chest where, between the nipples, the writhing serpent guarded the pierced, bleeding heart.

DUNCAN walked home through the late afternoon. The sky was overcast, but it was still hot in the wood. For Duncan, the very air was tainted with an appalling yet fascinating corruption. The heavy midsummer trees seemed to swell into strange, bloated shapes of sensuality. The subjects of Jim's photographs forced themselves, again and again, upon his over-charged consciousness. He reached home deadly tired, and went straight up to his bedroom. As he entered, his eyes lighted on the row of once-treasured objects on the window-ledge: the framed orchis, the photograph of his mother, the books, the skull, the handcuffs, a dried-up sprig of mistletoe. They seemed to stare back at him, now, with the unfriendly, vacant gaze of strangers.

Wearily he lay down on the bed and slept till supper-time.

NEXT day dawned hot again, with the same diffused sunlight, the same threat of thunder.

Duncan had slept badly; nevertheless, he rose early, and after breakfast walked up to the camp. The field, when he reached it, was a confusion of moving figures: tents and cooking-stoves were being loaded on to trucks, N.C.Os. and officers barked out their orders, soldiers in fatigue-dress were doubling back and forth amid clouds of dust. In the midst of this pandemonium, the stones rose grim and silent against the farther woods.

For an hour Duncan leaned on the hurdle, watching the scene curiously. He was afraid to go closer; and there was little hope that his friend would notice him in the confusion. Nevertheless, he continued to wait. After another hour, when he had nearly abandoned hope, he saw a familiar figure crossing the field towards him.

"Hullo, kid—what's up? Was you looking for me?" Jim's manner was nervous and rather suspicious.

"I only came to say goodbye," Duncan replied.

Reassured, the soldier grinned at him, and took his hand.

"Well, kiddo, it's been nice knowing you," he said, with a

vague geniality. "Daresay I'll run into you again sometime. . . . I'll have to sheer off now—the Sarge'll be looking for me. Cheerio, kid—good luck."

He was gone. Duncan watched him walk across the field, saw him absorbed again in the muddle of dust and khaki near the stones. Then he turned away and began to walk homewards through the wood.

Jim had gone; and it seemed to Duncan that, with his friend, he had lost his sole ally; henceforward, he would stand alone, single and powerless against the enemy.

BY the afternoon, the last truck had moved off, the last column had marched away towards Glamber. Duncan lingered about the camp, feeling tired and rather unwell. The hot, diffused sunlight beat down mercilessly upon the silent woods. Walking home again to tea, Duncan found a dead rook on the side of the path, and suddenly remembered Sims's curious warning: "They carry diphtheria."

After a late tea he stayed indoors; and at seven o'clock surprised Sims by saying that he thought he would go to bed. He undressed in the warm sunlight pouring into his bedroom; lay down, and was almost instantly asleep.

HE woke with a start of terror as his bedroom door was flung open. He must have slept for a couple of hours, for twilight now filled the room. He sat up with a jerk and stared into the gathering dimness.

There, in the doorway, stood Gerald: enormous and menacing in the half-light, his eyes dark with anger.

For a moment Duncan supposed it to be a dream: his uncle was not expected back till tomorrow. Then Gerald stepped forward: no dream, but a figure of flesh and blood, frighteningly actual. He paused at the edge of the bed, and looked down at Duncan's upturned face.

"Now just listen to me," he began, his voice harsh yet curiously tired. "I'm going to ask you a question, and I want a straight answer. It'll be better for you if you tell me the truth: God help you if you don't."

He paused, turned away towards the window, then turned sharply back again.

"Yesterday morning," he went on, "I had ten pounds in my note-case. When I got to the station, there were only eight. I'd counted the money, as it happened, just before I went to bed, as I'd paid out some to Sims, in wages. Now the question I want to ask you is: *did you take that two pounds?*"

Gerald had spoken with an unusual calm, which Duncan recognized as far more dangerous than his anger.

"Just answer me yes or no," Gerald added.

Duncan looked up at him, meeting his eyes with a calm, lucid honesty. He was alone now, fighting his own battle: it was war to the death between them, now, and Duncan knew it.

"Yes, I took it," he said, and lowered his eyes.

"Right," Gerald said, expressionlessly, and turned away again towards the window. He remained there for a moment looking out at the fading evening. Suddenly he swung round.

"I've done *my* damnedest," he exclaimed. "I've given you every chance; I've warned you again and again, I've let you off, I've trusted you. . . . And now this." He paused, then added reflectively: "As far as I can see, you're only fit for a Borstal institution."

For a moment more he stood there, his enormous body framed by the dim square of the window. Then he moved towards the door.

"Just stay where you are," he said briefly. "I shall be up shortly."

He went out, shutting the door behind him; and Duncan heard the key turn in the lock.

GERALD walked heavily downstairs. He had drunk a good deal in the middle of the day, and now felt intolerably tired. In the sitting-room, Sims was waiting for him: some household matter had cropped up. Settling it as briefly as he could, he dismissed the servant, and poured himself out a drink.

He drank it unhurriedly; then walked out to the shed and chose a cane. The drink had been a strong one, and he knew that he was walking unsteadily: he had not realized, till now, how much he must have drunk at midday.

In the sitting-room, Sims had laid a cold supper. Suddenly hungry, Gerald sat down and wolfed some cold mutton and salad; and at the same time drank a couple of glasses of claret.

Afterwards he picked up the cane; then put it down again. He would sit down for a bit first: it would do the boy no harm to wait a bit longer.

He must have slept, for it was dark when he awoke. His mind, struggling into consciousness, remained for some moments curiously blank. A tear-off calendar caught his eye, with the date in large red print: the twenty-third of June. The longest day: or was it Midsummer Eve? He couldn't remember which.

He got up unsteadily: he was sweating, and his head ached. The cane lying on the chair caught his eye, and memory returned. What I need is a drink, he decided; and, going to the sideboard, poured out a stiff whisky.

He sat down again. Outside the open window, the warm night seemed to be pressing round the house, heavy with menace. There was a low mutter of thunder in the distance.

He picked up the cane, and thwacked it gently across his knee. That little bastard upstairs: only fit for Borstal. Pinching fags, pinching money — and then lying his way out, or funking his punishment. . . . He'd have to be taught a lesson, once for all. . . . The doc. said there was nothing wrong with him: healthy enough, but highly strung. Highly strung my —— , discipline was what he needed.

Vaguely, Gerald's mind strayed backward over the past months. . . . I was fond of the kid, he thought; he'd the makings of a decent horseman; I could have made a man of him — but there just hasn't been the time, with the farm going to rack and ruin. . . . Then being expelled — nervy, hysterical. . . . Discipline, Gerald repeated to himself firmly: discipline was the thing.

He switched the cane sharply, again, across the side of his chair. The whisky was steadying him: his mind suddenly began to clear, like a landscape after storm. . . . Once, travelling by train in a strange country, he had noticed a range of hills on the horizon, and they had suddenly been perfectly familiar: every dip and hillock and escarpment was known to him. The very name of the hills had been on the tip of his tongue; and it had seemed of enormous importance to remember exactly when he had seen them before, to identify them. For days afterwards, the problem had pestered him; but he had never solved it. . . . Now, once again, it seemed to him that a landscape lay before him: familiar, clearly discernible as a contour-map, but in some way eluding definition. Directly he sought to find words for it, to pronounce the formula which would link each scattered promontory and valley into a coherent whole, his mind failed, and the vision retreated. At one moment the secret seemed as if it were on the tip of his tongue; at another, it seemed buried in a time and a world so ancient and so remote that a thousand years was as nothing to the immense span which divided him from it. Fleeting memories and phrases flashed through his mind, like will-o'-the-wisps, beckoning him with a spurious and misleading air of importance: something Duncan had said once about "voices" in a wood, and a light where no light could be; a dead chicken; a fragment of white cloth hanging on a bush; and that absurd date — today's date — printed in red on the calendar: the twenty-third of June. . . .

Gerald got up, stumbled to the sideboard, and poured out another whisky. The night seemed hotter than ever: oppressed, he took off his coat and collar, and unbuttoned his shirt. He was surprised, as his hand touched his chest, to notice that the flesh felt cold.

Moving heavily, he picked up the cane, and walked unsteadily up the stairs. The house was silent: Sims must have gone to bed. With a slow deliberation he switched on the light in his own bedroom; then went to the door of Duncan's room, unlocked it, and threw it open. His hand fumbled for the switch, which was behind the door; at length he found it, and, half-dazed with the sudden brightness, stepped clumsily forward.

The room was empty.

Gerald stood there, balancing himself unsteadily, for a full minute. His brain refused fully to grasp the situation. Duncan had been locked in; he couldn't have got out. Yet he wasn't there. . . . Gerald went to the open window and looked out;

but the dark moonless night revealed nothing. Turning back, he looked quickly under the bed; then returned to his own room. Immensely tired, he would have liked to undress there and then, and get into bed. Instead, he made his way downstairs.

With difficulty he found a torch and went out into the garden. Under Duncan's window the earth was disturbed, and a strand of creeper had become dislodged, and hung limply against the wall. A thick, branching wisteria rose to the height of the window: it was perfectly evident how Duncan had made his escape.

Gerald returned to the house, mounted to the top floor and called Sims. He moved more steadily now, and his mind was functioning coherently if slowly. Sims appeared in pyjamas, and Gerald gave a brief, incomplete explanation. Together they went downstairs, and returned to the garden. For half-an-hour they toured the garden, orchard and out-buildings, calling Duncan's name; but without result.

"It's a funny business, sir," Sims mumbled, as they returned to the house. "The boy went up to bed quite early — said he was tired. I should never have thought he'd have gone out again."

"What's the time?" Gerald asked.

"Close on midnight, sir."

"Well, we can't do much more. He'll be in soon, no doubt. I'll wait up for him — you go to bed."

Sims, after some argument, obeyed. Gerald, returning to the sitting-room, poured out another tot of whisky and sat down before the fireplace: his eyes fixed upon the open window and the crouching, inimical darkness.

A VAST field receded into the fading daylight: in its centre, a human figure lay transfixed and helpless. Across the plain, other figures were spread out in a rough circle, from whose circumference they could be seen to converge, with a slow, deliberate motion, upon the figure in the centre. It was impossible to tell whether the advancing figures were human or otherwise: they had limbs and the power of locomotion, but their gait was ape-like and irregular, and their faces, if they had faces, were invisible. Very slowly, with a horrible deliberation, they shambled forward towards the central point; each figure, as it advanced, could be seen to leave a silvery trail of slime, like that of a snail, upon the ground. Nearer and nearer they crept to the helpless creature in the centre; the far-flung circle gradually contracting, until the dim figures coalesced into a perfect round. The now-unbroken ring continued to diminish, centripetally, until the prone figure was hidden from view. . . .

Duncan woke with a stifled scream: something heavy and prickly was pressing upon his face. He struck out with both hands, and rolled over the edge of the half-built haystack, on to the firmer ground.

At first the darkness seemed absolute; then, with a kind of relief, he noticed that the stars were shining dimly, through a veil of cloud, but none the less he was able to pick out the Great Bear and Cassiopeia. As his eyes accustomed themselves to the blackness, he could perceive the shapes of objects, outlined dimly against a sky which, if not less dark, was slightly less opaque. There, beyond the stack, the stars were masked by a towering bulk: the stones. Beyond, on the field's edge, the line of the wood showed ebony against the sky's black gauze.

Gradually memory returned; the locked door; the knowledge that the long siege was over, that battle was joined at last; the clumsy, frightening descent from the window. . . . He had run aimlessly for an hour: anywhere to get away from the house. With a vague, irrational hope he had made at last for the camp: the home, till this morning, of the only friend he had in the world. . . .

The haystack, half-built, lay beyond the stones. Exhausted, he had climbed on to it, and slept — for how long he couldn't tell. Now, sitting on the dew-sprent grass, he began to feel chilly: he wore only pyjamas, with a pair of flannel trousers pulled over them. He got up, and walked vaguely up the field towards the stones. Between the two uprights, a stone slab, about the size of a large tombstone, lay embedded in the ground. Clutching the thin jacket around him, he lay down on the flattened stone, and waited for the dawn.

THE first cocks crew, and as though at a given signal, a small chilly wind rose, dispersing some of the night's heaviness. A long rustle like a sigh passed through the brooding woodland; a sudden gust banged the sitting-room window shut, waking Gerald in his chair by the fireplace.

He sprang up abruptly, as though unwilling to admit that he had slept. Mechanically, he reached out his hand for the cane; it was not there. Then he remembered: he had left it upstairs. In place of it, he seized hold of a riding-crop which lay near at hand, and, reopening the french window, stepped out into the garden.

It was still dark; but a faint pearly bloom lay over the east. Gusts of wind stirred the garden fitfully, and struck a chill through Gerald's half-clothed body. He breathed deeply, and pulled his shirt more widely open, letting the coolness strike his bare chest.

Soon he began to feel much better. He was no longer conscious of being tired; he could move steadily; and his brain seemed remarkably clear. He walked round the house, then made a tour of the farm. The east was brightening now, the stars gradually vanishing. Gerald walked out of the gate and started up the path towards the field where the camp had been.

An extraordinary calm descended upon him: it was like awaking from some nightmare. The dawn brightened over the woods; birds twittered intermittently; the dew was heavy on the grasses. In the west, a bank of purple cloud hinted a threat of thunder; wisps of grey cloud scudded untidily overhead; but to eastward the sky was pure and empty, the colour of mother-of-pearl.

Gerald struck at the hedgerows with his crop, walking forward with a sense of predestined certainty. Knowledge and purpose were strong in him: the mysterious landscape had revealed its secret, the missing formula had been spoken. As he reached the hurdle, at the top of the path, the sun rose: pouring its sheaves of light across the woods, the sloping field, and the great grey stones.

Gerald paused at the path's end, looking across the field: he thought he could detect a patch of fluttering whiteness between the stones. He climbed the hurdle, and strode across the dew-drenched grass, his trousers flapping in the wetness.

Duncan lay on the fallen slab between the stones: he was asleep, but he slept uneasily, his face was flushed, and he breathed irregularly. Gerald stood for a moment looking down at him, in the chilly sunlight. Then he leaned forward and grasped his shoulder.

Duncan's eyes opened, and for a moment he stared sightlessly up at his uncle: the next instant, he began to struggle like a wild animal in a silent agony of terror. It was like trying to seize hold of a fox-cub or a stoat; his whole body seemed filled with a wild, vindictive energy, mindless and unscrupulous.

Gerald tightened his grip; but Duncan, wrenching himself suddenly free from the loose jacket, slewed his head round with a quick, savage movement, towards his captor. Gerald felt a searing pain in his wrist, as the boy's teeth met in the soft flesh above the artery.

Maddened by pain and an uncontrollable fury, Gerald flung him forward brutally upon the stone, and, lifting the crop, brought it down again and again, with the full force of his muscles, across the white, boyish shoulders. At last, he felt the taut body go limp in his grasp: Duncan lay prone across the stones, motionless, his head dangling loosely in the drenched grasses. Panting, Gerald leaned over him, supporting himself against the nearest upright; blood from his wounded wrist fell in a dapple of scarlet upon the boy's naked back.

Wearily, he stooped over the prostrate body, and shifted it into a more decent position. Bending lower, he gently kissed the pale, dawn-chilled face; then, unhurriedly, laid his hand on the smooth flesh above the heart: knowing, before he did so, that it had already ceased to beat.

From far away, at the barracks over towards Glamber, came the faint nostalgic note of a bugle, sounding reveillé. Gerald turned away, seeing everything clearly at last: knowing that the long initiation was over; the rites observed, the cycle completed.

Recently I bought an old reference book called *Living Authors*. (A companion volume is less recklessly titled: *Authors: Today and Yesterday*.) It was published in 1931 and contains a biography, a bibliography, and a photograph or drawing of 400 "contemporary literary personalities, ranging from the great figures of our age down to the young poet or novelist with his first ('promising') book." The introduction goes on to say: "Posterity, no doubt, will forget many of these 'living authors,' but we need not be apologetic for our interest in them today. A mediocre living author is likely to impinge on our consciousness more than a good dead one." Posterity has indeed forgotten many of these authors, yet their books linger.

Books are objects; they are more plentiful and durable than the flesh that creates them, and so they remain in the world far longer than writers, or even the reputation of writers. When a book goes "out of print" we tend to think of it as being irredeemably lost or at least temporarily unattainable, but this is not really so: the many copies that were published do not disappear. Books that have lost their ISBN numbers and jackets are oftentimes easier to find, and cheaper, (and better) than those books that are officially "in print."

Denton Welch is one writer whose work seems to constantly hover on that forever fluctuating border of in and out of print. He is forever being rediscovered to no lasting effect. I started reading his novels that were, or had recently been, in print (*In Youth Is Pleasure,*

Maiden Voyage, and *A Voice Through a Cloud*), and then I searched out what more I could find, and bought an edition of *The Denton Welch Journals*, published in 1952 (a complete and unabridged edition was published in 1984), and *Denton Welch: Extracts From His Published Work*, which appeared in 1963. Both of these books were edited by some- one named Jocelyn Brooke, and as the only Jocelyn I had ever known was a girl in my sister's class at school, I assumed this Brooke was a woman, an assumption that seemed corroborated by the slightly ma- ternal tone of the introductions. At about this same time I read a book (*Tales Out of School* by Benjamin Taylor) published by Turtle Point Press, and wrote an admiring and thankful letter to the pub- lisher; a consequence of that letter was my being asked to write an introduction for one of the "lost" books they were publishing, a book called *The Scapegoat* by Jocelyn Brooke. I didn't immediately put the two names together, but when I did make the connection, it seemed a felicitous link. (It is sometimes strange how and when books come to you — by chance or by design, they often seem to ap- pear just when you are ripe and ready for them, as if there were some sort of master plan.)

So I began reading *The Scapegoat*, still assuming its author was a woman. This assumption was immediately challenged by the intense homoeroticism that is introduced in the book's first chapter, when Duncan is affected by the soldier's pungent masculinity. And then with the appearance of the almost preternaturally erotic Gerald March, I began to wonder about this Jocelyn person. I had pictured this editress of journals and literary extracts in tweeds and pearls, but then I vaguely remembered reading in Michael De la Noye's biog- raphy of Denton Welch that Jocelyn Brooke attended the same pre-

paratory school (St. Michael's) as Welch. And there was, I also remembered, some autobiographical mention of having served in the
army in one of the introductions. So it became clear to me that Jocelyn Brooke was a man, and the entirely and intensely masculine
world of *The Scapegoat* began to make more sense.

I can think of only a few books whose entire cast of characters are
all of the same gender, excepting those books about soldiers, or cow-
boys, or girls at boarding schools, and usually even in these books
there is a token character representing the "opposite" sex, to add
some relief, or throw into relief, the overwhelmingly masculine or
feminine world. But there are no women in *The Scapegoat*: Duncan's
mother dies before the book begins, and is never remembered with
any specificity. Gerald mentions a "daily girl from the village" but
she never appears and her presence is unfelt. Duncan moves from the
"inviolably feminine" world of his mother's house to Priorsholt,
"exclusively a house of men," and he makes this transition just as he
is entering puberty, as he is assuming (or being assumed by) his sex-
uality.

It seemed obvious to me that both Duncan and Gerald are ho-
mosexuals, or have, as is sometimes said, "homosexual tendencies."
Duncan has an active subconscious homosexual life, with his "phan-
tastic" island of exiguously costumed boys and men, and if one reads
between the lines — or sections — it appears as though Duncan may
have an active homosexual life as well. What are we to suppose happens in the half-naked soldier's hot tent in the "space" that separates
the final sections of Part Two, chapter six? We are pointedly told that
Duncan arrives in the field "after lunch" and departs in the "late
afternoon." We leave him in the tent, his ardor aroused by Jim's

pornographic photographs, watching Jim stroke his naked, tattooed chest. (Jim's tattoo visually echoes the splash of blood that earlier dripped onto Uncle Gerald's chest, "making a zigzag scarlet streak across the white skin," thus connecting these two erotic objects.) When we rejoin Duncan after the elliptical section break, he is walking home, "deadly tired," in a sort of post-coital daze. "For Duncan, the very air was tainted with an appalling yet fascinating corruption. The heavy midsummer trees seemed to swell into strange, bloated shapes of sensuality." It is clear what Duncan wants from the soldier, and I think that he gets—or buys—it.

Gerald appears to be more successfully repressed than his nephew, although one wonders who he visits on his frequent trips to London and the neighboring "pleasure town." Gerald is a wonderfully pitiful character: the inevitable disintegration of his magnificent body ("the fold in the belly, the slackening pectoral muscle"), his abject friendlessness and subsequent loneliness, his failure as a farmer, his solitary tippling, his ineffectual decency, and perhaps most poignantly, his inability to rehabilitate, to "make a man" out of Duncan. All of this is human, and complex, and dramatic. One feels less pity for Duncan: his stunted dumbness, both verbal and moral, prevents him from completely engaging the reader's sympathy. One wishes he inhabited himself a little less drowsily, yet while that might make him a more engaging character, it would make him a less convincing adolescent.

If the ending of *The Scapegoat* was not so unrelentingly tragic, one could almost read the book as a romantic comedy, for don't Duncan and Gerald pass amusingly (and arousingly) over and around numerous hurdles and into the same bed? If their circumstances were altered—if they were not both men, not uncle and nephew, not adult and minor—the reader would, I think, be wholeheartedly rooting for them to cohabit (some readers may root anyway). Yet despite these three imposing strikes against them, they manage to have a fairly conventional, Tracy-Hepburn, courtship: the morning jerks, the mistletoe, the fireside rubdown, the fireworks, and the conveniently rain-soaked bed, which leads to the bed that is finally, inevitably, shared.

I was very curious to see what would transpire in that bed. Gerald enters the room to find that "Duncan lay motionless as ever, his pyjama-jacket had slipped across his chest: he looked extraordinarily vulnerable, evoking in Gerald a sudden, peculiar sense of power. Seldom or never in his life before had he felt that any human creature was so entirely at his mercy. . . . In some remote hinterland of his mind, he was aware of danger threatening: it was like the first suspicion of some hereditary taint, creeping insidiously upon the healthy, normal consciousness." Duncan wakes, startled, from his dream of being attacked by weasels in the hellebore-wood, to see Gerald "sitting there in his shirt, his enormous white thighs hanging over the bed's side." And then Gerald assumes his "frogged silk pyjama-jacket" and the bed, where, "under the bedclothes he felt for Duncan's hand and squeezed it again." Duncan lies in the darkness, "disquieted by the proximity of his uncle's body," and his heretofore carefully separated real and dream worlds begin to merge. He has a premonitory vision of "a cold, stiff body, somewhere far from home in a great boundless field."

And then comes what I consider to be the pivotal gesture of the book: "The boy moaned in his sleep, and turned over, pressing himself unconsciously against Gerald's body." Something interesting happens here — or rather, fails to happen: "Gerald shifted to the edge of the bed, turned over, and tried to sleep. But sleep would not come. At last, after an hour or so, he climbed gently out of bed, put on his slippers and dressing-gown, and stole guiltily downstairs." In the dining-room he drinks whiskey and "for a long time sat motionless, staring into the cooling grate." We are not told what he is thinking. The narrator, who had supplied the reader with a long internal monologue of Gerald's before he enters the bedroom, abandons Gerald's internal world as he departs. The reader can assume that he is thinking of his nephew's warm body pressed against his own, but the narrator remains silent. (This silence seems more like an omission than an ellipsis to me.) Instead, we are given Gerald's subconscious thoughts; we are given a dream. I resist dreams in literature: they always seem too easy, the writer's way of spelling out in symbolic terms what has failed to be conveyed in the narrative. Gerald dreams he is hunting Duncan, a pursuit "fraught with an increasing sense of guilt and terror." He awakes from this dream "possessed by a creeping disgust, a sense of degradation which is like a physical nausea."

Guilt, terror, disgust; this is hardly the first (or last) time these emotions have been aroused. A sense of foreboding is introduced early on in the book when Gerald feels "a premonition of misfortune" immediately upon seeing Duncan's face in the arriving train carriage, and Duncan, upon encountering Gerald, feels "a disquieting sense of lurking danger." It is thereafter referred to almost constantly, and the sense of impending doom is as prevalent and intense as the sexual tension. When I first read the book I was perplexed and displeased with the overt and insistent portentousness of *The Scape-goat* — it seemed heavy-handed, unnecessary, strained. I wondered why Brooke chose to develop so much of the book on this vaguely ridiculous symbolic level; it seemed a throwback to Hardy when so much of the book seemed to be looking forward. It bothered me less on my second reading because I realized how difficult, how unacceptable, it would have been for him to tell this story on the simply human level, focussing as it does on the triple bugaboos of homosexuality, incest, and pedophilia. But if the desires and actions of these risky (and potentially repellent) characters are made to seem preordained, beyond their control, Duncan and Gerald are, I think, more readily acceptable to the common, mid-century, reader.

In the smug revisionary way we cast our glance back over literature, I wish Brooke had been more concerned with the humans and less concerned with the Gods, for the preordination seems to diminish, rather than enhance, the book's effectiveness. But the fact is that books are written when and by whom they are, and as there is no changing that, there should be no wanting to change that. It seems to me that the drama and doom are unnaturally heightened in this book, but who am I to say? Drama and doom are only, after all, a matter of perspective. And for a book written where and when it was, *The Scapegoat* is almost unbelievably subversive and kinky. It's no wonder that Duncan begins to have problems separating fantasy from reality, for the world of Priorsholt is every bit as titillating as his ultramontane "innermost sanctuary." What does a boy need a fantasy island for when he's told to "undress and get into bed" by his hunky uncle and waits there for him, naked and writhing in handcuffs? Yet in a world that neither acknowledges nor tolerates homosexuality, there is little happiness and no safety in either fantasy or reality. Gerald and Duncan are doomed by both the suppression and the expression of their urges, and that is the real tragedy of *The Scapegoat*.

I bought *Living Authors* because I hoped it might tell me something about Jocelyn Brooke, but it did not (Brooke was born in 1908 but did not publish until 1948) and his name is missing from all the other mid-century literary encyclopedias I consulted. (This is what I mean about authors disappearing more permanently than their books.) Finally, in Anthony Powell's pleasantly gossipy collected memoirs (*To Keep the Ball Rolling*), I found some interesting information about Brooke. (The reminiscence of Brooke is found in *The Strangers All Are Gone*, the final volume of Powell's memoir.) Powell met Brooke through the coincidence of their both (favorably) reviewing the other's work. It was literary friendship, sustained through frequent correspondence and infrequent meetings. In terms of biography Powell tells us that Brooke "was born in 1908 and came on both sides of his family from wine merchants." As a child he was passionate about botany and fireworks, subjects that he later worked dexterously into the narrative of *The Scapegoat*, and many of his other books. He ran away twice from King's School, Canterbury but eventually graduated from Worcester College, Oxford, of which Powell tells us "he afterwards retained only dim memories, and seems to have been a fairly typical Proust-Joyce-Firbank-reading undergraduate." Before joining the RAMC at the beginning of the second war, Brooke worked in a London bookshop, labored unsuccessfully in the family's wine business, and suffered "some sort of breakdown." As a soldier, because he "felt after a time that his life was too easy," he volunteered for the branch treating venereal disease, in which he served both during and after the war. Powell's comment that "Brooke always seemed to me to have resolved pretty well his homosexuality in life" is not elaborated upon, and *The Scapegoat* is the only of Brooke's five novels Powell does not mention. It is an odd and perplexing omission, especially as Powell comments on "the hint of mutual homosexual attraction, faint but perceptible," in another Brooke novel (*The Image of a Drawn Sword*).

Jocelyn Brooke died in 1966 at the age of 58, fifteen years before his three autobiographical novels (*The Military Orchid, A Mine of Serpents*, and *The Goose Cathedral*) were republished in one volume as *The Orchid Trilogy* (with an introduction by Powell, which repeats verbatim much of the Brooke reminiscence contained in his memoir). "In spite of having died comparatively young Jocelyn Brooke realized himself as a writer," Powell concludes. "He said what he had to say in the form he wished."

Readers of *The Scapegoat* may wonder if that is true. Elliptical in content and formally contrived, *The Scapegoat* does not seem to me a book written by an author saying what he has to say in the form he wished—and therein lies its peculiar appeal. As we move further and further (one hopes) from the time when homosexuality was condemned by society, books like *The Scapegoat* will become curiouser and curiouser—and more and more intriguing. In one of my novels I have a character, who enjoys having rather pointless theoretical discussions with her friend, suggest that with the relaxation of societal constraints, the tensions that once complicated great novels no longer exist. She contends that a rigidly constraining and moralistic society that discouraged homosexuality offered better fodder for great fiction than a society that tolerates homosexuality. I hadn't read *The Scapegoat* when I wrote that scene, but it seems to be a perfect example of the kind of book that my character may have had in mind. I can think of few books that are as erotically and dramatically charged as *The Scapegoat*, or that depict so convincingly the degenerative effects of sexual repression. Repression and suppression invariably result in tension, which is good for novels but bad for lives. In *The Scapegoat*, repression leads to the death of the heart and to violence. It is a "bad place," a "dead sheep, far gone in rottenness."

Peter Cameron
Author of *Andorra* and *The Weekend*